DEATH TRAIL

They had given Arizona Ranger Morgan Starret a mission—to find out all he could about the gun shipment being made to the Apache renegade Geronimo. But he wasn't ready for Catalina Gomez or her sophisticated lover, businessman and killer, Louis Bonnard—or the blazing guns and trail of death that followed.

DEATH TRAIL

DEATH TRAIL

DEATH TRAIL

by
Elliot Long

Dales Large Print Books
Long Preston, North Yorkshire,
England.

British Library Cataloguing in Publication Data.

Long, Elliot
  Death trail.

  A catalogue record for this book is
  available from the British Library

  ISBN 1-85389-698-5 pbk

First published in Great Britain by Robert Hale Limited, 1995

Published in Large Print January, 1997 by arrangement with
Robert Hale Limited.

Dales Large Print is an imprint of
Library Magna Books Ltd.
Printed and bound in Great Britain by
T.J. International Ltd., Cornwall, PL28 8RW.

ONE

Driven at its usual steady speed the prison van for Yuma neared the narrow pass through the hills. There was no rush, decided Deputy US Marshal John Hayes, who was riding shot-gun—despite this edgy feeling he had. Nightfall should see himself and the driver Charlie on their way back to Tucson—the scum in the cage behind them delivered.

He squinted at the Arizona sun overhead —a white, fierce ball battering them with its heat, and pulled a face. God, man, but it was *hot.* He lowered his gaze again and reached for his red, polka-dot handkerchief and mopped his brow while looking at the walls of the pass ahead, beginning to crowd in on the trail.

Inexplicably, as he stared at the gap—for there was no good reason for it as far as he could see—the feeling of nervousness in him grew stronger. There had never been any trouble here before. But this time he found some gut-deep instinct working on

7

him. He couldn't get away from it. On this trip—he shifted uncomfortably in his seat—those narrow walls seemed to exude a kind of dark menace.

He nudged Charlie, who was passing time practising flicking his long bullwhip an inch above the lead mule's ear.

'I know it sounds screwy, Charlie,' he said, his voice like rattled gravel, 'but somethin' ain't right up there.' He indicated with his shot-gun towards the narrowing of the trail.

Charlie raised brown eyes, webbed with laughter lines and set in a face that was as seamed as a walnut. It was a steady, but inquisitive stare. 'Like what ain't right, fer instance?' he demanded.

Hayes shrugged, waved his gun again, for emphasis this time. 'I dunno,' he said. 'I jus' feel somethin' bad's goin' to happen.'

Charlie eased up with the bullwhip and gave him a long, old-fashioned look before he spoke. 'Well, maybe *you're* thinkin' that, but I'm thinkin' the worst thing that's goin' to happen to us this day is that one of these bastards behind'll be wantin' to crap purty soon. It's been a long time. And, by God, *that* can be a real bad experience.' He indicated his meaning with a chuck of his head at the five men in the cage behind him, a wry smile spreading across his face as he did.

Hayes gave Charlie a disgusted look. 'Damn it, I'm bein' serious,' he said. 'I got this "ain't-right" feelin' up my spine.'

Hayes watched Charlie's smile ease off. The driver squinted his eyes. 'You ever thought about retirement, John?' he said abruptly, seriously, raising his right eyebrow.

Hayes's glare was questioning. 'Now what the hell's that supposed to mean?' he demanded.

Charlie spat brown tobacco spittle to the trail and rolled his wad to the other cheek. 'Nothin', really,' he said. 'On'y I knowed a fella onc't, 'bout yore age, he git all jumpy—like he was seein' a gun poked his way every turn in the trail. Well, he stuck it out fer a spell, said he'd git over it, said he'd tangled with that kind of feelin' before. But the sad outcome was, he finished up in a mental institution back East.'

Hayes glowered and reared up irately. 'He did, huh?' he growled. He waggled a finger. 'Well lookit here, Charlie, there ain't nothin' like that wrong with me, I can tell you that.'

Charlie rolled up lazy eyes. 'Ain't sayin' there is,' he said. 'Jest sayin' it happens to some people.'

'*Some* people, huh?' Hayes growled, nodding his head vigorously. 'Well, them *some* people ain't me.'

With that he glared forward with irritable silence, watching as the pass drew nearer until its walls closed right in on them. Despite the cushioning effect of his high resentment however, Hayes could not prevent himself stroking his longhorn moustache nervously with his left hand while taking a fresh grip on the stock of his shot-gun with his right. This damned feeling he had just would not go away.

He listened to the sound of the iron-shod wheels on the rough ground as the noise began to echo to and fro across the rocky pass. Well, he'd heard that sound plenty of times before, he conceded grumpily to himself. It shouldn't be a need for concern. But maybe Charlie was right; maybe he *was* getting too old for the damned job...

Being confronted with the possibility

Hayes rocked moodily in his seat. He found he still hadn't convinced himself it might just be he was past his best. But, damn it, a man should keep alert—keep wary; take notice of his hunches. The gut feelings he'd had had paid off plenty of times in the past. And the office had warned him there might be trouble. He hitched in his seat and stared gloomily ahead. But, then, they always did that...

At his side Charlie was leaning over once more, preparing to expectorate on the trail again when he gave out a short, gasping grunt, then stiffened. And in that split-second of time, the boom of the heavy calibre rifle rang out above them, sending sudden, tearing noise racketing into every nook and cranny of the pass. And Hayes found the racket sent raw fear jarring right through him.

But he was even more surprised when Charlie—in that same mesmerizing moment—pitched sideways, towards his side of the van seat, cannoning into him heavily as if he had been propelled by a powerful, invisible force. Then, without another sound, except for a kind of long sigh, Charlie slumped down into the foot well.

Then Charlie's head began to roll with the motion of the prison van. It was hanging over the edge of the foot board, his body in an awkward, precarious position in the well. And Hayes saw Charlie's eyes were staring up blankly at him, but clearly seeing nothing, for Charlie was dead. And the reins that had been in Charlie's hands were now trailing on the ground between the mules.

Then an unguided van wheel hitting a rock in that crowded couple of seconds flipped the wagon up and Charlie toppled out to hit the trail with a heavy thud.

With all these things going on in so short a space of time—the truth, when it came, was like a slowly unfolding nightmare to Deputy US Marshal John Hayes. But when it did become reality to him it sent adrenalin pumping through his veins, unravelling the knot of alarm biting at his gut and the immobility of disbelief that had come to his limbs.

And coming desperately alive from his momentary shock and dismay, he bawled at the mules to run and hoisted up the shot-gun and crouched and stared madly up at the rimrock with blazing eyes. And as he raked his grey stare across the skyline he grumbled anxiously, 'Damn it! I knewed it all along!'

Then he felt as though his head was exploding as the next bullet from the ambush rifle tore into his face, smashing his teeth and ripping his flesh and thumping him backwards out of the driving seat.

Though bemused and riven with shock by the violence of the event he still gripped the shot-gun instinctively, even though he hit the ground heavily. The blood from his wound splashed out of his mouth in a spray.

Ignoring his pain, his fighting blood rushing up, Hayes struggled to a sitting position on the trail. He raked the rimrock again with a fierce glare, attempting to sight the shot-gun as he did. But he never did feel or hear the shot that tore off the top of his head, or see the person that sent it his way.

Now, without any incentive from Charlie to drive them on, the six mules towing the prison van slowly came to a standstill on the trail and looked stupidly ahead, heads low and waited, the flies already coming down to feast on Charlie's and Deputy US Marshal Hayes's bloody corpses.

TWO

With the other four prisoners in the cage at the back of the van, Morgan Starret reared up from his seat, his hand and leg chains rattling as he did. He gazed around, massively alert, stunned by the suddenness of the violence and death that had visited them here.

He stared at the two bodies on the trail, and he wondered if the secrecy of the plan that had placed him in this situation had been blown, and it was now his turn to face the music. He felt slightly sick realizing that Deputy US Marshal Hayes and Charlie had gone to their deaths not knowing why they had, because of the judged need for this total secrecy from higher up, the philosophy being the less people who knew about the scheme to find out about the gun-running to the Apaches, the better.

And thinking more on it, Starret clamped his thin lips together to form a grim line. Personally he hadn't liked the plan from

14

the start; planting him, an Arizona Ranger, in Yuma Prison to dig for information to counteract the strong rumour brought in from good sources that a parcel of guns was to be run to that crazy Apache Geronimo pretty soon.

Starret rubbed his chin nervously. Well, already the plan began to look as though it was a dead duck. Had there been a leak? Not all men were pillars of society if the pile of dollars for a loose mouth was high enough...

Now Starret's anxious stare found the rifleman who had caused the mayhem. He could see him rising from the rimrock some hundred feet above the trail. The bushwhacker began to pick his way down the steep side of the pass, threading his way through the big boulders.

Starret could also see the big calibre Sharps in his hand. He narrowed his eyelids. Yeah, well, it figured, judging by the severe wounds inflicted on Hayes and the driver. Those big bastards could knock over buffalo at God knew how many yards range he'd heard. Damn near out of sight, some said.

But Starret's gut tightened even more when he saw the four horsemen starting out from the bend ahead—though, realistically, he decided, it was only to be expected.

But the man next to him in the cage, when he saw them—the prisoner Starret knew as Con Soam and the man he had to work on to find out what he knew about the gun-running rumours—let out a whoop.

'That's Louis Bonnard, Morgan,' he crowed. 'I knew he wouldn't let me down.'

Starret felt Soam nudge him like a pal. And Starret didn't mind. He had encouraged it—would have to continue to do so until...

But the name Soam had blurted caused Starret to narrow his eyelids. Louis Bonnard...now that was a name he'd heard of often in Tucson, though he didn't know the man. Clean as a whistle as far as he knew. As a matter of fact a respected businessman in the territory and beyond, so he'd heard. What he was doing here, and Soam's claiming him as a friend, was sure a turn up for the book.

Starret heard Soam rattle his irons in an attempt to lift his hands to wave at Bonnard. 'Louis, you great big sonofabitch!' he hailed. 'I knew you'd come.'

16

Starret could see the riders coming towards them were clearly hardcases, except for the one he guessed was Bonnard. They were all grinning wide and hearty as they rode up. Bonnard, though, Starret figured, must be the fine-looking one in the long duster coat and the expensive-looking stetson and cravat. He had a look of refined culture about him, alien to these parts.

On approaching Bonnard smiled at Con Soam in acknowledgement of the owlhoot's enthusiastic greeting.

And as he drew close he said, 'You banked on that, did you, my friend?'

Soam grinned more widely, thrust his manacled arms up against the bars. He crowed, 'Just you git these chains offen me, Louis, is all.'

Starret watched Bonnard continue to grin at Soam. He leaned forward in the saddle, his slim hands resting on the horn. Then the smile slowly faded from Bonnard's square face. 'Well, now, Con, just why should I do that—take the chains off you, that is?' he said innocently.

Surprised, too, Starret saw the big smile on Soam's face slowly fade and a look of puzzlement replace it. Soam licked his

17

lips and flicked a nervous glance at the other riders before returning his gaze to Bonnard.

'What the hell you mean, Louis?' he demanded.

Starret watched as Bonnard moved his right hand under the duster to pull out a long-barrelled Smith and Wesson American.

With a surprised gasp Soam stepped back in the confines of the cage, shock and terror coming to his eyes. In his haste he tripped over his trailing chains. His stagger stopped when he hit the bars at the other side.

'Now hold on, Louis, fer God's sake!' he said. 'What you intending here?'

'A little bird has told us you sold me an' the boys out, Con,' Louis said softly. 'Sang like the canary, we heard, when the law leaned on you. Your life for ours. That was the deal...OK?'

With a habit, cultured since early youth, which always sorted alternatives, second chances, despite the situation he was in, Starret's quick glance saw the rifleman who had been on the rimrock had reached the bottom of the pass. He was now making straight for Marshal Hayes, lying dead on the trail. He watched the rifleman immediately begin searching the lawman until he came up with the ring of keys.

Turning away from the distraction, seeing no real value in it, Starret saw the colour had now completely gone from Con Soam's face. And Starret found *he,* too, didn't know what to make of the development here. For Con Soam was the little bird he had hoped to make sing. But why this couldn't have been done at headquarters, Starret pondered again, left him slightly bewildered. He had considered it a crazy mess from the start. More so now.

But he didn't make the rules, make the decisions, he just carried out some of their damn-fool ideas. But, relieving the tension that had risen in him, he decided this holdup wasn't about him at all—as he initially thought it might have been.

He saw Soam's thin, cracked lips had started to tremble; saw a tic had begun to tug at his left cheek. He held out his manacled hands imploringly.

'Hell, Louis,' he said, 'you got this all wrong. I never coughed up nothin' about you, or our operation. Not a damned word. I jest cooked up a story to get me off the noose. They bought it.' He clasped the bars. 'Damn it, I didn't want my neck stretched for a killin' I didn't do. You can't blame me fer wantin' to avoid that, can you? An' I figured maybe you'd try to spring me, seein' as I know Geronimo an' can talk to him an' finish off this gun deal for you.' Anxious hope struggled up in Soam's eyes. 'They ain't come after you, have they?'

Louis shook his head. 'Not yet,' he said.

Soam gripped the bars. 'So it's like I told yah, ain't it?'

Stunning Starret with its sheer unexpectedness, Bonnard's Smith & Wesson exploded with noise. The bullet from it hit Soam in the midriff and Soam screamed once then gave vent to a despairing moan. He hunched over, his manacled hands clutching at his guts.

Starret could see blood immediately begin to ooze through Soam's fingers. On legs that were clearly already becoming shaky, Soam sat down on the same part of the bench he had only recently vacated to stand and clutch at the bars and cheer Bonnard.

His face now twisted up with pain he

gasped, 'Fer Christ's sake, Louis, I swear to God I never said anythin' about you.'

Bonnard nodded, his face was calm and composed. To Starret's shocked gaze, it looked as though Bonnard could have been on a Sunday outing for all the shooting had affected him, and Starret could not miss the cold look of contempt in Bonnard's amber eyes.

'I know that, Con,' Bonnard was saying evenly. 'But I heard tell you did warble a little, enough to get Johnny Spain arrested and taken into Tucson for trial.'

'He doesn't know nothin' about you, or runnin' the guns to the Apaches,' said Soam, whining pleading now in his voice. 'He don't amount to nothin', anyway. You allus said you could never trust him knowin' about the big one 'til we came right down to doin' it. You allus said that was why you had him and the other boys rustling on the Texas border to keep them occupied, out of the way, until the main operation was all set up.'

After his whining Soam groaned with pain and stared at Bonnard, defiance and loathing in his eyes. 'Now, Jesus, God, you lousy bastard, after all that,' he protested, 'you've kilt me!'

21

Thinking over the top of Soam's cussing Starret narrowed his eyelids, his attention coming alive to hear the information in the previous words. So it was true...it was this trash who were going to run the guns to Geronimo. Damn it, had he hit the jackpot in a most unexpected way? Or was he the next to be gunned down?

When he looked at Bonnard again, the bastard was nodding slowly, smiling at Soam. 'That is right,' he said. 'But, don't you see, Con, even now you are running your mouth off, as, I think, the American term is. I explained to you on numerous occasions it was always your weakness. So who's to say that next time—if I'd have allowed you to live, that is—you wouldn't have gone and spilled a whole lot more...maybe for remission time? They say Yuma is one hellish place to spend seven years in. You gave them Johnny Spain...could I risk you giving them me?'

'Damn it, Louis, this whole operation was my baby,' whined Soam. 'I thought up the whole deal.'

Bonnard smiled and shrugged. 'Yes,' he said. 'It is true. Pity. But, that's life, Con. Right?'

Soam moaned his despair and sagged.

Starret resisted the man's body, which was now leaning hard against him. Coldly he stared up at Bonnard.

'You gonna leave him like this?' he said.

Bonnard turned narrow, deeply-searching amber eyes on him, as if seeing him for the first time. After long moments of looking he said, 'Why not? I want him to know what it is like to spill his real guts...'

Starret blinked at the cold, dispassionate nature of this man on the big horse, staring at him through the bars. Louis Bonnard was, for sure, purely some cool, murderous bastard dressed up in fancy businessman's clothing. And clearly now it appeared Bonnard was involved in the things he, Starret, had been planted in the van and Yuma gaol to find out about. Word had come—from God knew where—of the impending gun shipment to Geronimo. Once more the murderous renegade had broken out of San Carlos and was waiting in the hills to receive it the story went.

At the thought Starret licked his parched lips, felt his gut churn, looked around him and fidgeted with his chains. This Bonnard seemed a cruel, ruthless man for sure. 'So

23

what about the rest of us?' he said.

He realized Bonnard's amber gaze hadn't left him—it was still hard and glittering as it studied him, but now also curious. 'OK,' he said. 'You lookin' for work...?' It was then Starret noticed the slight accent in the voice.

He shrugged. 'I can allus use a buck. Especially now.'

Because of Bonnard's question, Starret felt a stir of cautious optimism. Seems, maybe, he wasn't in line for shooting, and that Bonnard didn't know why he was here. If he could get Bonnard's confidence...

'What are you ridin' the cage for?' Bonnard was saying.

Starret let his even stare hold the gang boss's narrow, quizzical gaze. There had been a rehearsed plan. 'They say I killed a man,' he said.

Bonnard's dark, thick brows lifted a little, knitted. 'And did you?'

'No.

Bonnard smiled briefly. 'Of course...but the law says you did,' he said, disbelief heavy on his voice.

'Right.' Starret attempted a grin, too. 'With the element of doubt, the judge said life.'

Soam let out a cry of pain and toppled forward, away from Starret. Starret could see blood was red on the bench seat and the bottom of the cage where Soam had been sitting. Despite the chains holding him, Soam was now curling up in the foetal position on the cage floor, his manacled hands pressed tightly into his gut. He was moaning all the time now.

Cold anger burned in Starret as he lifted his gaze again to meet Bonnard's stare. And the quick thought raked like a spur across his mind. Even though Soam was a no-good sonofabitch, from what he'd gathered, he didn't deserve to die like this.

Starret held down the loathing he was feeling for this ice-cool, amber-eyed killer before him. Surely, the day would come when justice would be meted out to Bonnard.

'So where do we stand?' he asked again, indicating the others in the cage this time.

Bonnard relaxed, grinned—affably, it seemed to Starret, disgusting him—and let go of his gaze long enough to stare at the other prisoners.

He said, 'Well, the fact is I'll be

lookin' for good replacements now Con isn't feeling too good and Johnny Spain is out of the picture.'

Starret watched as Bonnard turned to the bushwhacking rifleman standing nearby on the trail. He had the marshal's ring of keys in his hand and was looking quizzically at his leader.

'OK,' Bonnard said. 'Let them loose, Joe, while I think about it.'

As Bonnard said the words, Con Soam vomited. Starret watched as bright blood flowed from the suffering man's mouth. After it was over Soam started moaning again, rolling and holding his gut and muttering, 'Jesus, God', over and over.

Arnie Friedman, another of the prisoners —sentenced to three years for stage robbery and assault upon the person, Starret understood—stared up at Bonnard. 'Damnit, like Starret said, you gonna leave him like this?' he demanded.

Bonnard's gaze was hard as it turned on to Friedman. 'What do you want me to do with him?'

Friedman glared. 'The man's in bad pain,' he rasped. 'He ain't goin' to live. You know very well what I mean, damn it.'

Starret watched Bonnard's amber gaze narrow, turn murderous again. 'But you haven't the guts to say shoot him, yes?' he said. 'You'd be advised to keep quiet, my friend, OK? I don't take kindly to people tellin' me what I ought to do. Do you understand that? But I will tell you this—whatever I do, I do for a purpose.'

Friedman seemed about to say more, still glaring up, but the Smith & Wesson trigger was being cocked again, expressively. Friedman's face went long, pale and hollow. His indignation died very quickly. He shuffled, his ankle chains rattling.

'Well, guess it ain't my business,' he said grudgingly.

Bonnard grinned slowly, the aura of menace that had swiftly cloaked him when the challenge to his intentions and his nature had been made, fading. 'You've been persuaded on that, huh?' he said.

The incident clearly quashed, Starret watched as Joe unlocked the cage door and began undoing the wrist and ankle chains holding all of them, apart from Soam.

When freed of them Starret rubbed his chafed wrists and climbed stiffly out of the cage with the others. Standing on the trail, the overhead sun beating down on him unmercifully he said, staring up at Bonnard, 'So what about that job?'

'What are you good at?' Bonnard said, narrowing his eyelids questioningly. Starret again detected a slight foreign accent.

'I've used explosives,' he said. 'I know my way around guns. Been on a few heists.'

'OK. So you are telling me you are in the business?'

'Had a few posses on my tail.'

'What's your name?'

'Morgan Starret.'

Bonnard looked cautious, suspicious. 'The name is not familiar.'

'I've always worked alone, until I took on a weasel-mouthed pard—'

'Ah,' Bonnard interrupted.

Starret shrugged, looked down at his prison garb. 'Well, I reckon this is the consequence of that,' he said, decorating his statement with irony.

Soam—his moaning cutting in on the conversation again to Bonnard's clear annoyance—got up from the floor of the cage and leaned against the far bars. Then Starret watched Soam stare with agony-filled eyes through the cage bars at Bonnard. Blood dribbled from his mouth.

'Damn you for a murderin', thievin' sonofabitch,' he screamed, 'hit me out of it, will you!'

Starret saw the plea had made little impression on Bonnard. The well-dressed businessman with the faint foreign accent turned away. He said to him, as though the conversation hadn't been interrupted, 'I see...er, Starret. So, how did the murder charge arise?'

'It was pinned on me.'

'By whom?'

'My weasel-mouthed friend an' partner, who actually did it.' Saying it, Starret flicked a glance towards the stricken Soam before returning it to Bonnard. 'Maybe a bit like *your* friend here in Johnny Spain's case,' he said. 'If what you say is true.'

Bonnard nodded slowly. 'It's true,' he said.

Now Starret watched Bonnard hitch in the saddle, lean forward. It seemed to Starret the man's stare—now boring into him—was endeavouring to reach into his very soul. 'Well,' Bonnard said after moments, 'as I mentioned, I can use good men.' His stare continued—long and hard and probing before he spoke again. He said, 'OK. We'll see how it works out. Come along with us. You can double up on the buckskin with Joe.'

Prompted by that and wanting to establish the impression he was as good a hardcase as the rest of them, Starret turned to stare at the riflemen. He nodded. Joe nodded also and looked narrowly, but neutrally, back at him.

When Starret turned back he could see Bonnard now had his attention centred on the moaning Soam. 'OK, Con,' he said. 'You win, I suppose. I've listened to your noise long enough.'

The noise from Bonnard's gun startled Starret again. And he watched with horror as the force of the bullet smacked Con Soam back against the cage bars. Now Starret saw the slug had drilled a neat hole plumb centre of Soam's forehead before it shattered his brain pan at the back and spewed out brains and blood through the bars.

Soam dropped, his legs trembling and stretching out across the cage floor—sliding through his own blood, the chains still on him rattling harshly with the reflex movements.

Starret turned up steely eyes to become aware the gang leader's amber gaze was on him again. This man, he decided, was a dangerous killing machine who, it seemed, got his loyalty through fear.

'That all right with you?' Bonnard said.

Starret fought to calm himself, though it was he who had first suggested Bonnard put an end to Soam's suffering. Now it was done. But he wouldn't, couldn't show his true emotions, or show sympathy for Soam. He must try to appear as ruthless as Bonnard. Which, in truth—as he had proved on an occasion or two in the past—he could be if what he did was in the name of Arizona justice.

'You dealt the cards,' he said. 'Guess you've finished the play.'

He watched Bonnard's eyelids narrow, his amber gaze continue to stare before he replaced the Smith & Wesson in the holster under his duster.

'OK,' he said. 'No complaints, huh? I'm warming to the feeling that perhaps we'll get along well, you and I, Morgan Starret.'

Still that faint accent, thought Starret. French? Maybe New Orleans? He'd been there once. Heard some of the accents.

Now Friedman, his face thin, his gaze

narrow and suspicious, and seemingly unaffected by the shooting, said, 'You got Starret fixed up, Bonnard—what about us? You got somethin' fer us? I've run hot cattle into Mexico, held up stagelines.'

Starret watched Friedman, as he spoke, sullenly motion towards the other prisoners standing around in the hot sunlight with him. There was Preese, the woman killer. Shaney Gaunt...

Starret blinked. Well, he didn't know much about Gaunt. Child rape had been mentioned, and he had nearly been lynched for it.

Now he watched Bonnard look at the three prisoners, one at a time, then shake his head. 'Sorry, I got nothing for you, boys.' He rubbed his square chin, faintly blue with stubble. 'And the trouble is...you being here, seeing this, knowing what we are about, too, since Soam spoke of it... I can't let that go, either. You understand?'

Starret, suddenly made tense and alert by the words, watched as Friedman's narrow cheeks drew in with stark alarm as he realized their message, too.

The stage robber stared at Bonnard disbelievingly. The other two—Preese and Gaunt—did likewise. Preese even clawed for a non-existent gun.

Friedman, now clearly grasping at straws, said desperately, 'Now hold on, Bonnard. We're all in the same game. Dammit, you know we won't talk about this. If there ain't nothin' here, I'll be headin' for Canada. I tell you, you got nothin' to fear from me.'

As if he hadn't even heard Friedman, Bonnard half-turned in the saddle. Over his shoulder he said, 'What do you think about it, boys? You know how I feel about security right now.'

Starret tensed as he watched Colts being drawn by the other three horsemen. Joe, standing nearby, was lifting the big Sharps Starret knew to be lethal in his hands.

'Jesus H Christ!' Preese moaned. 'Fer God's sake, you can't do this!'

Then Preese, clearly deciding they could and that pleading was not going to earn him any compassion, turned and started running down the pass. Almost as soon as he did Joe's big Sharps boomed out.

It brought a despairing cry from Preese. The bullet sent him hammering forward before he collapsed, blood spurting from his mouth. He sprawled headlong into the loose sand and gravel on the pass bottom. Then he lay trembling—one hand reaching forward, grasping a handful of dust before it, too, became still.

During this, Gaunt also took to his heels, but Friedman showed more spunk. He ran at Bonnard, cursing, and made a grab for the sleeve of the gang leader's duster, to pull him out of the saddle and take his gun.

But Bonnard, his lips drawn back off his clenched, even teeth, evil in his amber eyes, brought his right boot up and thrusted it at Friedman's chest, sending the owlhoot staggering back to sprawl on to his backside in the dust.

Then Starret saw Bonnard's hand slide for his Smith & Wesson again, under the duster. When it came level the shot from it sounded crisp and clean amid the other shots from the other three owlhoots as they brought down the fleeing Gaunt.

Helplessly, Starret watched as Friedman's open, oath-spitting mouth gushed blood where Bonnard's bullet smashed into it, before the lead went on to shatter the spinal column. He watched now as Friedman died, staring straight into the sun, his destroyed mouth still attempting to form cuss words.

The business over as quickly as it had

begun, Starret took the slaughter grim-faced, fighting to force stoicism and calmness upon himself.

When he brought his gaze away from the bodies he became aware that Bonnard's gun was on him. And Starret tightened up, swallowed on an incredibly dry throat.

'I thought we'd come to an arrangement,' he said, as coolly as he could.

Bonnard nodded, smiled. 'OK, that's right,' he said. 'And it still holds. You fit into my plans. Lucky for you, huh?'

Starret, now full of cold, simmering loathing for this murdering bastard, relaxed as best he could. Bonnard was definitely a man you didn't fool with. He was a killer with a brain.

'Yeah,' he said. 'Lucky fer me. So, what now?'

'We ride,' Bonnard said amicably.

Starret nodded but he didn't answer. He couldn't. Though he strived to hide his seething anger he knew that his grey stare must be giving his feelings of disgust away.

But Bonnard smiled that slow smile he had and stared down at him. 'You don't like what's happened here, do you, Starret?' he said.

Starret blinked. He'd give this bastard so

much, no more, choose what it cost him or the Department. There were some horizons a man just didn't cross over if he called himself a man.

'No, Bonnard, I don't. It's bloody murder.'

To Starret's surprise, Bonnard nodded, smiled. 'OK,' he said. He leaned forward, his gaze now calm and neutral. 'You may not believe this, Starret, but I like a man to be honest with me. I thank you for it.'

Then he turned his big roan in its own space and urged it west, up the pass, with a cruel dig in the flanks. 'OK, boys,' he called. 'We go back to the canyon...Starret, get up behind Joe.'

As Starret swung up, dark apprehension closed down on him. He didn't know where the hell this was going to lead him.

THREE

After a night camp in the hills, mid-morning found Starret and Bonnard's men riding through broken country. And Starret became alert sitting behind Joe. He watched as they

36

entered the narrow, hidden gap in the sheer rock face behind the screen of conifers they had been climbing steadily towards for the past hour from the dreary, dust-dry flats.

After a hundred yards of narrow confine the trail broadened out into a lush little canyon. Under cottonwoods, by a slow-moving stream, he could see two well-built adobe cabins. A woman was standing by the door of the largest one, smiling. Other women were washing laundry by the stream or were staring idly from several shack doors also built here, some standing with their watchful, hardcase men. There was the crisp ring of steel on an anvil, too, which diverted Starret's gaze to the farrier's place a couple of hundred yards up the creek. Pale smoke rose from the furnace. He could see a big, leather-aproned man swinging his hammer, a big dun horse waiting to be shod. This was a veritable little robbers' village here, decided Starret, but he received no sense of permanence as he stared at the dwellings—from the shacks, anyway, the adobes, maybe yes.

As the party rode into the shade of the cottonwoods and dismounted, the woman standing on the stoop of the largest adobe came forward.

Starret could not help but gaze at her; she was a strikingly handsome woman. Tall, straight-backed, with green, direct eyes gazing out from under arched, thin brows. Her Titian hair, not done up, hung down to the middle of her back giving her a certain, he suspected, intentional, untamed appearance.

He watched as Louis Bonnard dismounted and had his horse led away. Then Bonnard took the woman in his arms and kissed her with surprisingly tender passion for long moments. But though the woman pressed urgently to him, Starret realized, with a slight feeling of intrigue, her eyes were on *him,* peering over Bonnard's big right shoulder, curiosity clearly in her gaze.

When Bonnard let her go she stepped away a little and nodded towards him and said, while coyly playing with Bonnard's cravat, 'Who ees that?'

'Morgan Starret,' Bonnard said. 'He'll be with us from now on.'

'What does he do?' A brow arched up.

With a smile Bonnard took her arm and led her towards the larger cabin. 'Let me find that out later, honey, OK?' he said. 'No inquisitiveness now. You should know it is always first things first with your Louis.' He pulled her close to him, his arm around her slim waist.

The woman laughed throatily. 'You never let me down, Louis,' she said. She stroked his square chin. But she turned to Starret. 'Perhaps we will talk later, *señor?*'

'Maybe, ma'am,' Starret said. Her accent suggested she was Mexican, but seeing her haughty demeanour and challenging eyes, there was still a lot of Spanish blood in her.

He pulled his gaze off her and turned it on Bonnard. 'I need clothes...'—he looked at the prison garb they'd given him to wear—'a gun.'

Bonnard's amber gaze flicked over him. Question marks were in it. 'We'll work on it later,' he said.

Starret wanted more than that. He didn't like this feeling of naked vulnerability the absence of a gun at his hip gave him, particularly in this den of thieves. But the owlhoot boss didn't seem concerned about the matter and led the woman away towards the largest of the adobe cabins.

Beside Starret, Joe—whose second name was Bell, he'd informed him on the ride

39

here—said, 'Guess you'd better bunk down in there fer now.' He nodded towards the slightly smaller adobe building further along the creek from the large one. 'Thet's the cabin we, the regulars, use.'

Starret said, 'Bonnard's got quite a little army here.'

'Twenty men, not includin' us,' Joe said. 'The rest—eight—on the Texas border, rustlin'. He's got these people here just for this one big deal he has comin' up.'

Starret pursed his lips. 'Don't it beat it? You just never can tell. From what I've heard around Tucson, I allus understood Bonnard was a legit businessman....'

Joe grinned. 'Yeah,' he said. 'An' most of the time, I guess he is. You will learn that Louis Bonnard is a strange man, Starret. He remains unknown to the rustlers he employs regular on the border; avoids them because he thinks maybe they'll spill on him sometime. For sure, he don't need to employ them—fixed well as he is in stocks, cattle dealin' an' silver minin'.'

As he looked at him Joe screwed up small grey eyes and shrugged. 'Seems the man just has to do it; he just has to be doin' somethin' on the edge. Maybe gives

40

him a boost of some sort. I don't know. Like it's in his blood an' he can't get rid of it. He keeps us four'—he nodded at the other three men who were in the party at the pass, and now busy with their horses—'for kind of persuasion jobs, you could say. You know, people a bit slow in payin', or gettin' in the way and wantin' removin'.' With that comment, Joe grinned more widely.

Soaking up the information like blotting paper Starret said, curious, 'You been with him long?'

Joe's brown stare went sharp, alert for a moment before it took on the look of affability again. 'No harm to know, I guess,' he said. 'From early in the war. He's French. Chased out o' his own country, they say. Good family. Officer from the French Army, but down on his luck. His one-time thirst for gamblin' brung that on, so the story goes. Some said, when the talk was strong, there had been a killin' involved—duel of some sort—an' thet's why he ran. He's the kind that let's all sorts of crazy tales revolve around him, so long as they don't clash with this odd sense of honour he has. You'll maybe run into thet before long.

I guess he figures what he did to Soam a real hoot, aside from Soam breakin' trust, that is. Soam settin' up the deal with Geronimo, settin' up where to get the guns....'

At that Joe chuckled and spat. 'Once, in a moment o' weakness I guess, for Bonnard's usually close-mouthed about his past, he told me he came to this country lookin' fer action. Well, by God, he found that a'right. Got to be captain near the end, though—in the Confederate Army, o' course.'

Joe spat and squinted his eyes, looked as though he felt he might be saying too much. However he went on, 'During the war they gave him all sorts of dangerous jobs to do. He asked for them, crazy bastard that he is. Well, I guess he picked up this need to pilfer from the company he kept during that time in the war...Quantrill, as did us all.' Joe pursed his lips and shook his head. The pause made Starret realize Joe's grey stare was now searching his own steady gaze. 'Does that name say anythin' to you?' he queried.

Starret nodded. It sure did. William Clark Quantrill, born in Ohio, former Kansas schoolteacher, notorious leader of a Confederate guerrilla band. The man who put Lawrence, Kansas, to the torch leaving 150 dead and 200 houses destroyed, amongst numerous other murderous deeds. Yes, he sure knew who Quantrill was.

Joe sighed and waved an arm, as if now tiring of the tale. 'Well, to cut a story short, for two years after the North-South business was over we heard nothin' from Louis and never expected to again, though he did promise he would contact us. We all kind of went our separate owlhootin' ways. But, damn it, he did send for us. And we bin with him ever since.' Joe turned and indicated with a nod of his head to the other three riders. 'Me, Clute James, John Rigo and Harlon Pheasy.'

Starret said, 'I figure you shouldn't be tellin' me this—Bonnard wantin' his identity clean an' all...'

Joe shrugged. 'It ain't clean any more, is it?' he said, as if he resented it. He nodded towards the shacks in the canyon. 'He's got this big thing comin' up, needs that scum over there.' Joe shook his head. 'Well, hell, I think Louis's gone crazy, tangling with this one. They're nothin' but a nest of

43

blackmailers in the makin' over there, is my guess.'

Starret immediately felt inclined to agree. It was an odd thing for a man like Bonnard to do; a man who had gone to considerable lengths to maintain and protect his anonymity—exposing himself only to men he felt he could trust implicitly, the bond of that trust forged in the fires of war. This camp destroyed all that.

After his long speech Joe turned, stripped off his saddle and smacked the buckskin into the fenced pasture alongside the creek.

Staying with him Starret said, 'This gun trade...when and where, d'you know?'

Joe smiled. 'He'll tell you that if he reckons you need to know. I'll show you Soam's bunk. You can use that.'

Rested, shaved, washed down and possessing Soam's Colt and Winchester, which he had cleaned meticulously (the possession of which had been suggested by a now relaxed Bonnard, after spending the afternoon with the Titian-haired woman) Starret walked out into the cool night full with a supper of hot Mexican food.

At the corral by the creek he reached

for the makings he'd found with Soam's things and formed a cigarette. He lighted it. Soam's possibles had been useful all round except for one thing—his smaller-sized clothing hadn't fitted Starret, so he still had to wear his prison garb.

The woman came quietly out of the night almost before he had put his arms out to lean on the corral rail to appreciate the tobacco and the dark, moonlit reaches of the canyon he stared down.

'I am Catalina Gomez,' she said. 'I am Louis's woman. Thees afternoon, you were watching me. Maybe, some day pretty soon, you will want to make me *your* woman, yes?'

Taken aback, Starret stared into the green eyes studying him through the silver dark. 'What gives you that idea, ma'am?' he said. 'I ain't here to poach another man's woman.'

A ghost of a smile played tantalizingly on Catalina's plump, inviting lips. She fluttered her long lashes. 'You weel not get away from me that easily, Señor Starret,' she said throatily, almost playfully and with a giggle. 'A woman like me knows thees theengs about a man, the way they look at her. She can feel it. No matter what you may theenk now, someday soon you weel want me for your woman.'

Made immediately alert by the potential danger in this woman, Starret said, 'You've got the wrong impression.'

Brief, mischievous light flashed in Catalina's eyes and the smile still played alluringly on her lips. 'You theenk so, Señor Morgan Starret?' she said. 'You do not believe thees facts I say, *si?*'

Starret pursed his lips, dribbled smoke out of his nostrils, allowed himself a small smile. 'I find it hard to, ma'am,' he said.

He decided he had to remain as cool as he could. Of all things he didn't want trouble with Bonnard over his woman, as pretty and as tempting as Catalina Gomez was.

'Plis,' she said. 'Not, *ma'am*. Catalina, yes...?'

Starret nodded. 'As you wish...Catalina.'

She laughed again, in that throaty way she had. 'You say eet nice,' she purred. 'And, *si*, I weesh you to.'

With that she came close—so close Starret could now smell the faint hint of expensive perfume being Bonnard's woman would probably allow her to afford.

'You find me...attractive, Morgan Starret?' she said.

He couldn't lie there, by God.

'Yes, Catalina, I do,' he said. 'You're a fine-lookin' woman. No doubt about that. Any man who can call himself a man would have to say so. But I guess you already know that.'

'All thee same, I like to hear eet—all thee time,' she said. Then her slim-fingered hand came up quickly and stroked his sun-leathered, stern face—gently, caressingly, sending tingles of fire scurrying through his body. Fires he could do without.

'And you steel do not want to admit you weel want Catalina Gomez as your woman very soon?' she cooed. 'Ha?'

Starret, though trying to fight it, felt irresistibly stirred nevertheless. It had been some time since he had had such close contact with a woman, and seldom a woman as beautiful and enticing as this one.

Holding his emotions on a tight rein he said, 'There is still the matter of Louis Bonnard.'

'Louis ees not always here, Morgan Starret,' she purred. 'And I am a woman weeth beeg appetites. Can you not see thees?' She stepped away momentarily, flaunting her curvaceous body at him, gazing at him, before crowding him again, the warm contours of her form surging fresh sensations of desire through him. 'Are you not a *man*, Morgan Starret?' she demanded.

Starret licked his dry lips, wrenching his mind away from the sexual urges now burning up in him. Damn the woman! he thought savagely. He did not want this. It was crazy! It was all crazy!

Even so he found the words hard to force out. 'Catalina, I ain't here to tangle with Louis Bonnard. He's goin' to pay my wages.'

She smiled some more, her facial skin olive-light and alluring in the moonlit night. She rubbed herself against him. 'But you find the idea attractive, do you not, Morgan Starret?'

Starret firmed his lips before he snapped, moodily, 'You know damn well I do, Catalina.'

She stroked her slim, smooth hand along his muscular neck this time, running it up into his dark, wiry hair. Fire thrust through him at her touch. Damn it, he thought, she was playing hell with him! Sweat began to bead on his forehead.

'Louis has gone away,' she said. 'He has beesiness. When he comes back, we start for Mejico. Before then, could we not make love, you and I?'

Starret fought to stave off her damnable enchantment.

He said abruptly, ignoring her suggestion, 'Mexico, you say?'

Catalina giggled. Her magnificent breasts lifted upwards as they pressed against him. She said, 'You do not know? Of course not. You are new. Louis ees careful.'

'So what happens in Mexico, Catalina?' he prompted. 'I've been told nothin'. And I'm a curious man.'

She hip-swayed coyly away from him and giggled some more. Starret felt his tensions relaxing immediately, her release of him relieving the temptations he was sweating under.

'And being eenqueesitive, you theenk you should be told, *si?*' she said. She raised her fine chin-line to the starlight. 'Morgan Starret... Louis weel tell you what he weel need you to know when he ees ready. Eet is not up to Catalina Gomez to do that.'

'Why not?' Starret demanded. 'I'm one of you now.'

She giggled some more. She came to him again, as if impulsively—so close he found the perfume on her was almost overwhelming in its titillation of his already aroused senses. Then, shocking him, he felt her hand grip his genitals and explore them gently.

'You big boy, *si?*' she said.

Starret felt hot urgency flood through him at her touch. He fought against it, angry he should have to. The woman was dangerous. And this had gone far enough. She was toying with him—God knew what for. He grabbed her hand and eased it away.

'I think that's enough, Catalina,' he said.

She laughed outright this time, bending her head back revealing her long, lovely neck arched and white against the faint light of the stars. Her sleek hair hung down to her waist.

'You theenk so, Morgan Starret?' she said.

With another giggle she broke away from him, abruptly, leaving him wet with sweat and breathing quickly—wrestling with the natural urges now aroused and surging through him. He found there was a primitive, almost irresistible allure about this exotic female that would drive any man to do crazy things. And he'd come within an ace thickness of succumbing to it, too.

And leaning against the corral rail, the starlight etching out her provocative bust she said, lazily eyeing him up and down, 'You have no clothes, Morgan Starret?'

He stared at her. A sudden anger filled him now, at her behaviour. He felt an overwhelming temptation to spank her. She needed it, disturbing him the way she had.

But he shook his head. 'No,' he said.

'I weel get you some,' she offered, as if spontaneously. 'That ees nice thought from Catalina Gomez, *si?*'

He nodded, finding the heat within him cooling quickly. He felt calmer now—even a little flattered by her erotic attentions, but still wary.

'Fine,' he said.

She giggled once more in that throaty, enticing way she had. Her green eyes were laughing at him. 'Goodnight, Señor Starret,' she said. 'You have sweet dreams *now* Catalina has...spoken weeth you, maybe?'

51

Maybe, hell, he thought. Out of the influence of her playful enchantment Starret found he was seething. Damn it, he had enough to think about, be aware of, without having Bonnard's woman playing cat and mouse with him, toying with him. Jealousy was a green-eyed monster he didn't want to run up against here, particularly where his mission was concerned.

Staring at Catalina's back he dropped his cigarette butt to the ground and stamped it out as he watched her walk away into the night. After moments, cooled again, he shook his head and smiled wryly to himself. Then he made for the smaller adobe *casa*. When he entered, he found Joe Bell looking up from darning his socks.

'Free air feels good, huh?' he said.

Starret nodded. 'Yeah, purty good.'

Joe grinned. 'She bin botherin' you?'

Starret glared at him. How did he know? The dirty bastard been spying?

'Who?' he said.

Joe cackled. 'Hell,' he crowed. '*Who*, fer Christ sake? Catalina, that's who. She eats young, good-looking fighting men like you for breakfast if she gets the chance. You can't tell me she didn't stir you up some down there.'

Starret resented Bell's knowledge, and that he must have probably witnessed Catalina's sensual attempt at seduction, if that was what it had been. He still wasn't sure. And, he thought sourly, could this now seemingly genial man be the same one that had shot down Marshal Hayes and Charlie the driver so cold-bloodedly?

'She tries it on, huh?' he said, falsifying a chuckle.

Joe looked up knowingly. He cackled a laugh. 'Hell, you know she does,' he said.

Starret flopped on to the bed that had been Con Soam's. This was a damned silly conversation. 'Sure, I guess so,' he said.

Why the devil was he bothering answering this man?

Joe rose and helped himself from the coffee pot simmering on the pot-bellied stove in the far corner, still guffawing.

Starret watched him, but he was in no mood to discuss Catalina or anything else with Joe. He turned over on the bunk, pulling the thin grey blanket about him. He was sore-eyed, bone-sagging tired.

'Night,' he said.

'Hell,' grumbled Joe, 'you're about as talkative as Soam was.'

Starret said, 'That the truth?' then he let sleep crowd in. He decided he was in no danger here...

Not yet...

FOUR

In the morning Starret found, despite her erotic playfulness last night, that Catalina was as good as her word, though the clothes she brought him were a mixture of Mexican and Anglo. Woollen trousers and shirt, concho-studded chaparejos, bolero jacket and small, black, low-crowned hat. Soam's gun and belt, though, hung easily and reassuringly about his hips.

He attempted a few practice draws with a fancy twirl return to leather. Joe Bell whistled admiringly from the corral rail.

'Says it all, Starret,' he commented. 'You don't need no armed guard.'

Starret said, 'When do you figure we'll be movin'?'

Joe squinted against the strong morning

54

sun. 'Impatient, ain't you?' he said. 'Well, cayn't be too long, I guess. Time's pressin'. Maybe tonight, if Bonnard gets back from whar he's bin.'

'An' that is?'

Joe stared. 'You think he tells me everything'

'Well, seems you're in good,' Starret countered. 'What is the big deal that's bein' cooked up?'

Joe let out an exasperated sigh. 'Jees, but you're a persistent cuss,' Then unexpected friendly warning came to Joe's look. 'In this neck of the woods, Starret, that can be mighty unhealthy.'

Starret stared, said gruffly, 'I just don't like uncertainties, Joe. Anythin' wrong with that?'

Joe waved an impatient arm, his look giving the impression he considered there'd been enough prying questions. 'Take my advice,' he said with warning in his voice, 'Bonnard'll tell you when he's ready to. Right?'

Starret lapsed into grudging silence and stared out into the canyon. All around he could see men working; men getting ready to ride. Hardcase men, clearly preparing for trouble. Well, it was no use pushing too hard, not yet anyway. He wasn't on firm enough ground. He decided to take a walk up the canyon.

Afternoon saw Bonnard's return to camp. Behind him—except for the squat, fierce-looking Indian riding with him, Remington cap-and-ball in his belt and clasping a Springfield carbine—trailed half a dozen Apaches in single file.

Seeing them, Starret's stare turned cold grey. He reared up from his seat on the stoop of the adobe cabin he, Joe and the others used. When he saw the brisk move Joe—who had been sitting by his side—grinned, looked up from the stick he had been whittling.

'The one with Bonnard,' he said, 'that's Geronimo.'

'The hell it is,' breathed Starret. Last report at Ranger headquarters was that after he had broken out of San Carlos reservation the Chiricahua medicine man had run for his strongholds in Mexico, leaving a trail of devastation behind him.

He watched the group disappear into Bonnard's large adobe *casa*. The meeting lasted over an hour. Then the Apaches appeared again, mounted and rode at a fast trot out of the canyon, Geronimo erect and fierce at their head.

For some time after they had gone, Starret continued to stare at the spot where they had disappeared—through the narrow passage that took them out of the canyon into the burning, ochre-coloured hills beyond.

Their appearance here had made Starret feel incredibly uneasy. He gazed at the point until Catalina approached with swinging hips, maybe five minutes afterwards. She came so close to him Starret could again smell the same enticing perfume she had worn last night.

'Louis wants you, Joe,' she said, while her lips and eyes smiled at Starret enticingly. But when she had delivered her message she went back with Bell, leaving Starret gazing after her, wondering what the hell the voluptuous Mexican temptress was really up to. Or was she just one of these women who liked to lead men on, sometimes, in the end, with tragic consequences?

Though it was difficult, he dismissed her from his mind. Catalina was a complication he could do without and wouldn't encourage.

But, thinking on the real situation here

caused raw impatience and concern to begin to start gnawing at him. For, Catalina aside, what the hell was Louis Bonnard up to—and had to be up to now he had finished off Soam, who, it appeared, had been doing the negotiating work until he was captured? Though Starret knew he hadn't a shred of evidence, apart from those few words from Soam back in the pass—the words, Starret now suspected, that had cost the owlhoot his life—he knew he had nothing except his own hunches and what Joe Bell had talked about yesterday. Damn it, if it was gun-running to the Apaches Bonnard was about he had to know the plan, then get out...if he could.

And what would be happening at Ranger headquarters? He knew Captain Mossman never had more than fourteen men under his command at any one time. And Mossman must know by now about the ambush of the prison van—the killing of Hayes, Charlie and the prisoners. And, Starret thought, Mossman must be wondering about what had happened to himself, too.

The appearance of Geronimo, here in Arizona again, was big enough news in itself to pass on. Knowing that the renegade was once more in the vicinity would be enough to cause anxious eyes to scan the horizon and send gnarled hands reaching for guns.

Just then, Clute James, another of the men who had been with Bonnard in the pass, spat juice on to the stoop boards. Starret realized James's brown gaze was studying him suspiciously.

'You seem kind of restless, Starret,' he said.

Starret gave him a quick, moody glance. 'I just don't like bein' in the dark,' he said curtly. 'That murderin' bastard Geronimo hangin' around here, too.'

As if relieved for some reason James grinned, scrubbed his grizzled sandy beard. 'Geronimo?' he said. 'Thet what's gripin' you? Hell, you fret none about thet Injun.'

Starret concentrated his full attention on to the owlhoot, now staring a little mockingly at him. Because of Joe's failure to be more forthcoming yesterday, Starret felt maybe he should try and prise something out of Clute James.

'You ever been on the bad end of an Apache raid?' he prompted.

James grinned. 'Once or twice,' he said, 'but never real bad. Shot me a few o' the

59

heathen, though—if that's whut you want to know. The price of a scalp can set a man up in whiskey and a clean woman mighty good fer a spell.'

'You seen what those bastards can do?' Starret persisted, not revealing his dislike for scalp-hunters.

'Hell, whut wanderin' pilgrim in this neck o' the woods ain't?' declared James as though he didn't believe Starret was asking him. He spat brown juice again. 'But, I tell you somethin', Starret: you ought to see whut me an' John Rigo here did to a couple of *them* poor innocents time back! Jees, d'you think *they* got the exclusive on givin' people a bad time?'

He rocked back in his chair guffawing before he let loose a rooster's call. Then he turned to the tall, lean, sallow-faced man clad in black, leaning against the door jamb behind him, whittling—John Rigo. Rigo was laughing, too.

'Yup,' Rigo said when the noise had subsided, 'I remember one o' them times in particular myself. The one Clute's talkin' about, 'smatter o' fact. Man, that was really somethin'. You bet. Was like this: we found these two squaws collectin' berries, mebbe a leetle too far away from their camp, see—up in the Mogollons, weren't it, Clute?'

James nodded, his face now expectant, his mouth—exposing yellow teeth—forming an open-mouthed grin.

'Well,' Rigo continued, 'they fought like wildcats fer a spell, but 'tweren't no good. By the time we'd finished with them they sure knew how a white man did it—before we scalped 'em, that is.'

Both he and Clute James burst into peals of fresh laughter and cockerel calls. When they subsided, Rigo said, 'So don't you go frettin' none 'bout them Apaches, Starret. We allus give as good as we git.'

Starret felt disgust fill him for these two men and their boasting, even though he had witnessed the terrible violations done to white women by the Apache. The plain truth of the matter was, in his book anyway, two wrongs didn't make a right, in that sense anyway. What you did do was hunt the murdering scum down and ship them off to Florida, that's what you did with Apaches. He stared moodily across the canyon to the ochre-coloured south wall a quarter of a mile away.

It was then Joe came back from visiting Bonnard. 'We move tonight,' he said looking round the faces staring back at him.

Starret growled, feeling frustration gnaw at him again. 'Where, damn it?' he demanded. 'I reckon I've a right to know.'

Joe gazed at him with steady grey eyes. 'Before you bust more gut, Morgan,' he said, 'Bonnard give me permission to tell you. It's Mexico.'

'Then what?' Starret insisted.

Joe grinned this time, raised sandy brows. It seemed to Starret, Bell enjoyed stringing him along. 'Well now, he didn't say more'n that,' he said.

Starret felt he wanted to punch Joe Bell, then storm down to Bonnard's cabin and demand the truth from him. But immediately he knew that would be about the most stupid thing he could do. For there was no telling how Bonnard would react to something like that and such inquisitiveness would almost certainly arouse his—as he had observed at first hand—already suspicious mind and murderous inclination.

No, Bonnard was not a fool, thought Starret, calming himself. He'd have to play along with this secrecy game to get to the bottom of what was brewing up here. And above all he had to survive to tell of it when the truth was discovered, for he felt this was something very big and very serious. If Geronimo was implicated in the gun running Soam had touched upon before he died—if the guns were for that devilish Apache...

At the thought Starret pressed his lips together, forming a grim, stern jawline. The consequences of that flashed horrendously across his mind. Burnt homes and murdered settlers, devastation and misery all the way to Mexico and beyond.

But why was Bonnard mixed up in something like this? Gun running. OK, there was money in it, but not big money—not the sort of money Bonnard was used to; not the sort of money that would profitably finance an operation as large as this appeared to be. There had to be something else behind it.

Something really worth Bonnard's time and effort, for, Starret felt, the Frenchman was, first and foremost, a businessman, with a businessman's need to show a profit. Even Bonnard's excursions into crime would have to pay handsomely,

Starret decided. It couldn't be all just compulsion, as Joe Bell had claimed it was, with Bonnard.

'I need a horse,' he said.

'There's a remuda a mile down the canyon,' Joe supplied. 'As a matter of fact Bonnard said cut one out and use Soam's saddle on it.'

Harlon Pheasy who had been sitting up the stoop, apart from them, quiet and dozing—the fourth rider who had been in the canyon with Bonnard—lifted his greasy stetson off his dark, swarthy face, which was vividly scarred in places. His nose was bent to one side, too, and had clearly been broken at some time, probably more than once. His dark, cold eyes stared up. 'Take my cayuse, Starret, unless you want to walk,' he offered.

James tittered suddenly, off to Starret's left. Starret attempted to ignore it, but knew it foreboded something. In a way, he found, he had been waiting for something like this to turn up.

'Obliged,' he said, flicking a brief glance at James attempting to seek clues. But the man was now blank-faced—but it looked as though he was having difficulty holding down his hilarity.

Starret knew Pheasy's mount was the stocky pinto with the deep chest, standing at the tie-rail in front of the *casa*. The scarred, taciturn owlhoot had ridden it from the pass of death yesterday.

His quick mind working on this new predicament, Starret reckoned Pheasy, truth be known, was the real rooster amongst this group of four, as well as the prankster.

And as soon as Starret approached it, the pinto wall-eyed him and moved nervously. Starret became even more suspicious of Pheasy's generous offer. But he couldn't decline the ride, not now, because he knew—*this was initiation time*, amongst other things. They wanted to know what steel was under his thick skin, if, indeed, there was any.

'He's kind of a one-man horse,' Pheasy said.

Starret grinned a grin he didn't feel. 'That's what he told you, huh?' he quipped.

The pinto stomped restlessly as soon as he gripped the reins and freed them off the tie-rail. With one agile swing he mounted and settled into the deep saddle.

Nothing happened for a second, then

the pinto seemed to explode. It started to mince forward on stiff forelegs first then began bouncing along on all four legs. Then it sunfished—three, four times, twisting like a whiplashed snake mid-air in the now dust-shrouded, hot air. The fourth time it landed it sidled swiftly with mincing strides and rammed its side against the wall of the adobe before rubbing along it, clearly bent on breaking his leg had he not removed it quickly.

But Starret hung on grimly, striving to play the part—though he'd never had any inclination to be a wrangler—whooping and beating the small black hat Catalina had given him against the maddened horse's rump. Damn it, he'd ride the beast if it was the last thing he did.

Now he rammed his heels in, urging the pinto to run, run the devil out of him, teach him that the man on its back was equal to anything a horse could throw at him and wasn't going anywhere until the contest for supremacy was resolved.

Three more sunfishes resulted, then four stiff-legged prances before the pinto ran on full tilt, then stopped abruptly.

Starret found the strain the sudden stop imposed on his thighs, back and arms was tremendous. He found himself lurching violently forward, on to the neck of the beast. But he clung on, stayed there—wrestling his way back into the saddle again, fighting the beast while soothing it, cooing to it, giving it the iron hand in the velvet glove; imposing his will on the resentful, lashing animal.

Now the pinto decided to charge up the canyon, running like the wind, its mane streaming back—a wild, spirited beast desperately wanting freedom from the alien man clamped on its back.

But, no matter what he did, the horse found the man was still there, stuck to his back like a leech—stern-handed, but coaxing, and definitely not for moving. Yet there was a gentle touch there, too, a gentle voice the horse discovered, a touch and sound he gradually found he didn't mind so much. The alarm in him calmed a little. He thought maybe, in the long run, it wouldn't be all that bad—being under the man who smelled and felt different from the one he knew, but didn't like so much. This man sat on his back firmly yet considerately, his strong thighs gripping his body so tightly but with consideration. No, this man was different to the other one...

Starret sensed a change in the beast, felt the pinto relax a little, ease down to a canter, then a trot, then stop. Now it stood in the shallow creek snorting and chucking its head, turning wild eyes up to look at him.

Starret allowed it a few moments to calm, stroking its quivering neck, talking to it easily, soothing it before turning it and sending it back towards the adobe cabin.

The pinto, now gentled, stood quietly when Starret drew rein by the hitching rail in front of the stoop. Clute James, Joe Bell and John Rigo gazed at him with grudging admiration.

'You mean like that?' he said, staring at Pheasy.

Harlon Pheasy growled, rose, looking ugly. 'Damn it,' he snorted, 'thet was a one-man horse.'

'You don't like him gentled?' Starret said innocently. 'Hell, you shoulda said.'

Pheasy started forward. 'You bein' smart-ass with me?' he grated. 'Well, lookit here, boy, you-all ain't goin' to take the shit outa me.'

Starret grinned, feeling flushed, his blood roused by his battle with the horse. The adrenalin was flowing. And he could now sense another type of fight was brewing up here, too. He decided he could do with it. The past two days had put a lot of frustration in his gut he wanted to be rid of—sexual and otherwise.

One thing he knew, a fight always relaxed him, straightened out the spikiness of his nerves. Second, with a victory, he could set the pecking order existing here to perfect right, he being established as the big cock-a-doodle-doo on this roosters' patch. And to be able to do it in one go pleased him more than some.

'Hell, I on'y reckoned on taking the shit out of the horse,' he said. 'You tellin' me you're full of horseshit, too?'

Pheasy, face contorted with fury at the retort, growled angrily and shouldered forward through the others ranged across the stoop. He came down the steps at a run.

Before Starret could evade the lunge he found himself unexpectedly caught and dragged from the saddle. But he managed a wrestle-hold on Pheasy as he dropped and rolled into the dust. But the force at which he hit the ground broke his grip.

Already a crowd had gathered to watch

Starret tangle with the horse, so this battle was a bonus to them. Raucous cheering started, urging Pheasy on. When Starret heard it, it became obvious to him the short-fused man wrestling with him was their champion, maybe through fear of him.

As soon as he hit the ground Starret rolled fighting to gain his feet, but he was surprised to see Pheasy's right boot was already swinging at him, so swiftly had the man gained his feet.

Starret paddled frantically away—evading it—his two hands working like a turtle's flippers behind him, propelling him through the deep dust. Startled by the ferocity of the assault he twisted, rose and circled, his two fists raised now, his grey eyes watchful.

Pheasy was chunky, thick-shouldered. He was clearly going to be a formidable opponent. And he watched as Pheasy adopted a prizefighter's stance—dancing and weaving, stabbing out with his left fist, seeking an opening.

But never the man to hold back on a fight long Starret stalked forward, swinging his right fist with bar-room abandon. But it cleaved thin air. Instead, iron-hard knuckles thumped into his own mouth and pain fired through him. He staggered back, jarred and confused—his hot, fighting blood surging through his veins as he tried to evade further timed, precise punches.

Pressed by the onslaught, ducking and sparring away from the rain of blows that were coming his way from Pheasy, Starret took further punches.

He knew he had to go on the defensive. He hunched into a peek-a-boo style, peering through his fists, waiting for his punch-fuzzed sight to clear.

He could see Pheasy was a grinning devil before him, prancing and weaving, whipping out swift, stinging punches that Starret felt thumping into his ribs and face no matter how he strove to fend them off.

Starret took them, breathing hard, thinking, looking for that opening he wanted, needed, the blood running from his nose streaking his dusty face with crimson and dripping off his chin.

He realized he couldn't feel anything. Not now. No pain. His fighting blood was rampant, dulling all sensation. All he was intent on was to inflict pain upon Pheasy—batter him into submission any way he could.

Then the chance came as Pheasy dropped his fists for a moment to taunt him, crook a finger beckoningly at him, point at his chin, inviting him to hit it, to the delight and cheers of the bystanders. Cold, controlled anger filled Starret to be so belittled as he peered through swelling eyelids. Stirred by Pheasy's arrogance he waited his time then stepped in swiftly, bringing his right up through Pheasy's momentary open guard to connect on Pheasy's chin. He felt it jar solidly on bone and flesh.

The arm-jolting punch caused Pheasy to grunt and stagger back, shaking his head. And with it Starret saw startled surprise cross Pheasy's scarred features, as well as pain.

Spurred by it, Starret went after Pheasy, hitting him this time high on the forehead, sending him backtracking, blood streaming from the deep cut inflicted upon his right eyebrow.

Cheered by his change of fortune, Starret now moved forward recklessly, wanting to finish it. But the fist came from nowhere again, slamming into his temple and sending him staggering backwards towards the creek, his head ringing with the force of the blow he had received.

And stunned again and looking through the red haze dulling his vision once more, Starret could see Pheasy weaving swiftly towards him, his own blood-streaked grin returning to his face, his guard open, his fists sparring for an opening, poised to do more damage.

Starret anxiously shuffled aside to try and avoid the menacing figure of Pheasy driving towards him with victory in his eyes.

Then Starret felt his boot catch on some driftwood by the creek and he found himself fighting to maintain his balance, pitching into the water, scattering the women there. He knew they had been washing clothes here until the fight had started—now they were shrieking, primitive females, their eyes made round and excited by the blood and violence created by two bloodied, battling males.

In the confusion, Starret found himself hampered by the floundering, blood-inflamed women scurrying around him, their wet skirts held high to avoid further soaking.

And Pheasy came in from nowhere again.

Starret felt his punch smack into the side of his face, causing him to cry out involuntarily. The force of it drove his head back. The glare of the sun momentarily blinded his eyes and water sprayed in a glistening cascade everywhere from his long, flared hair as he staggered backwards.

For moments he was aware of nothing, only confusing noise—of shrieking women and cheering men and himself splashing about in the water, bemused, disorientated and tottering.

Then he saw Pheasy once more through concussed, blurred eyes. The man was grinning and bowing and waving to the women and prancing about, sparring like the peacock he was.

Seeing the demonstration sent Starret's fighting blood coursing through him once more. Surges of new energy went pulsing through his numb, bruised body, renewing it. But he found he had to fall back on the deepest wells of his stamina to respond.

He came up out of the water like a raging bull. He'd thrash this prancing, arrogant bastard into submission if it was the last thing he did! He went tearing into the astonished Pheasy, battering through his hastily formed defence.

As he lashed into Pheasy, Starret found his spirits burning through him—a flaming, primitive savagery that wouldn't be quenched. And he found his blood-lusting emotions rejoicing with each pounding blow he drove into Pheasy's body.

Driven, he forced Pheasy back under a hail of blows. He sent them crashing into Pheasy, the impact of their force jarring through his arms, jarring against Pheasy's body and facial bone—burying themselves into Pheasy's slight paunch, sending the breath rasping out of the previously cavorting owlhoot.

And Starret drove on, not heeding the blows that were raining back at him...

It took him some moments to realize he was striking nothing, that Pheasy was no longer being driven remorselessly backwards before him, soaking up the blows.

Starret stopped, swaying with fatigue, his breath rasping out of an open mouth running with blood, slightly puzzled by the fact that Pheasy was no longer there. When he came out of the red haze he was in he found Pheasy was in the shallow water at his feet, propping himself up with one arm, shaking his head, water dripping from his long, dark hair.

Starret splashed forward, his wrath rampant. He made a grab for Pheasy, to inflict more punishment, but Pheasy fended him off.

'Enough, Starret,' he muttered through battered lips, raising a defensive arm.

For a moment, still in two minds whether or not to continue the beating, Starret stood there, then grunted, staggered away and flopped into the cool water himself a little further up the creek. Now he began to feel his own bruises and cuts. He, too, had taken one hell of a thrashing by the feel of it, he realized.

He lay in the cool of the stream, letting the water wash around him, swilling away the blood and the grime from the clouds of dust they had stirred up in their bitter battle.

Then he felt a hand on his neck, a soft hand. He opened his already puffing eyes to see Catalina. She had a whiskey bottle in her hand.

'Thees time thee bull win, not thee matador,' she said quietly, but with clear, joyful admiration for him in her tone. 'You were like thee big, black, rampaging *toro*, Morgan Starret. The sword of thee matador ees no match against the likes of you. That strutting prizefighter, Pheasy, he not ween thees time, no. He was finally met with the courage and fire of the bull. *Bueno. Mucho bueno*, Morgan Starret.'

Starret blinked and stared at her dizzily for moments while the information sank in. Prize-fighter? Pheasy was a boxer. He might have known. And greater pride surged up in him to know he had beaten him, fair and square. He gulped at the whiskey offered him. Its fiery fluid bit a way into his stomach. He coughed, but it was good.

He even managed a painful grin. Catalina's praise and interpretation of the fight he didn't quite know how to take, though.

'A bull, huh?' he said. 'Well, damn it, I've been called some things...'

He grinned again at the comparison, though it pained him to do so. He got to his feet slowly and splashed out of the water. He could see Bonnard was standing by the water's edge, staring at him with those amber eyes of his. The owlhoot chief looked impressed, though what emotion Bonnard ever felt was well disguised.

'Bravely fought, Starret,' he exclaimed, patting his wet back. 'You know, Pheasy was quite a prizefighter in his day.'

He turned to Catalina coming out of the water beside Starret. He put a pondering finger to his thin, wide lips. 'The comparison to fighting the bull, Catalina...I like it. Yes.'

Catalina flashed an even-toothed, white smile. She said, 'Eet is poetry, Louis. *Si?*'

Bonnard smiled and kissed her gently on the cheek. 'Poetry, *mon amour.*'

It was then Bonnard's admiring gaze lifted off Catalina, looked over Starret's shoulder. The amber brightness hardened. Now Starret became aware he was being pushed out of the way and that Bonnard was reaching and pulling the Smith & Wesson at his hip in the fancy black holster, fastened over his Prince Albert coat.

'Put it away, Pheasy,' he was warning. Then two guns rapped lashing sound into the canyon, echoing away through a thousand facets of ochre-coloured rock. Starret heard lead fizz past him.

Shocked, he spun, crouching, dove for his own Colt, but he knew he would have

78

been far too late. He could see Pheasy was teetering, gun hanging loosely in his hand. His dark eyes were staring disbelievingly at Bonnard, then he dropped to his knees, held on a second before he pitched forward and died.

Grim-faced, Starret turned and stared at the Frenchman, standing off to his left, still holding the smoking Smith & Wesson in his slim hand. After moments, when he had recovered, Starret said, 'Seems I owe you my life.'

Bonnard nodded, looked pleased by that. Then said, quaintly, 'Yes. That OK?'

Starret nodded warily. 'OK...but from what I hear, you, James, Bell, Rigo an' Pheasy go 'way back.'

Bonnard looked surprised. 'That is a strange reaction. The man was going to kill you in cold blood, Starret—from behind. A despicable thing.' His eyes narrowed. He slid the Smith & Wesson back into leather. He said then, 'Somehow, you don't fit, Starret. I'm getting a feeling about you. Do you think, for one moment, that I could tolerate such disgusting, cowardly behaviour from anyone—no matter who it is?'

As he spoke Bonnard's square, tanned face was deadly serious, his eyes questioning and intent. 'Discipline, Starret,' he barked. 'That is what I require. Discipline and obedience. Pheasy knew that. He was fairly beaten. He should have accepted it. Clearly, he couldn't. He paid the price. OK?'

Hearing the explanation Starret recalled Joe Bell had said something about Bonnard's odd sense of honour. Starret gazed steadily at the Frenchman, then raised his dark, cut and painful brows. He nodded. 'OK, I guess.'

Bonnard looked satisfied with that. He turned and raked his gaze across the other men on the stoop before he brought his stare back to Starret. 'So bury him,' he said. 'All of you.'

With that curt dismissal of the affair Bonnard turned, held out his arm. 'Catalina? Come.'

The Mexican firebrand linked with the proffered arm and with a proud toss of her head walked away with Bonnard. But Starret was embarrassed by her direct smile at him before she did.

'A bull, Morgan Starret,' she called. 'You are thee great black *toro!*'

FIVE

By nightfall Starret was busy preparing to leave for Mexico, trying to ignore his punished face and body. He was surprised when Catalina Gomez came to him and flashed one of her most alluring smiles.

He was standing outside the smaller of the two adobe *casas* fitting Soam's saddle and bedroll on to Pheasy's pinto. He had thought about leaving Pheasy's saddle on the horse but a woman who claimed she had had more than a passing relationship with Pheasy had demanded it be given to her, along with the rest of his possibles. She had stared at him defiantly when doing it, even suggested he see Bonnard if he had any objections. He didn't, he'd said. Why should he?

Catalina said, huskily, 'Louis wants to see you.'

Starret eyed her doubtfully. He had resolved to tread light around this lady, avoid her if possible. She was trouble he

81

didn't want. 'Sure it's Bonnard who wants to?' he said.

She laughed, throatily. 'Eet is a pleasent thought, my big handsome bull,' she said. 'Eet ees a pleasent thought you maybe want to pass some time weeth Catalina.'

Though it hurt physically to do so, he managed a cautious grin. Seems Catalina would try to milk every situation to hear praise for her many charms, he decided.

He said, 'Yeah, well, like I explained, Catalina, I ain't in the market right now. You're Bonnard's woman. Let it be like that. Now—where will I find him?'

She raised her finely traced brows. 'Een hees *casa.*'

Standing close by him while he finished what he was doing Catalina swayed alluringly on her ample hips, her arms akimbo while she gazed boldly, almost mockingly, at him. However, she didn't make further conversation and he was thankful for that.

His work on the saddle completed, Starret turned and without even a backward glance at her he strode off into the warm night, leaving her looking speculatively after him. And that surprised him a little. He felt sure she would have walked with him had

Bonnard wanted her in the cabin while they talked—if it was talk the Frenchman wanted.

But he felt good. As he strode along he looked up to appreciate the night sky, framed between the canyon's rims. He could see the moon had yet to rise but the Milky Way threw a jewel-sprinkled banner across the dark Arizona sky.

Inside the large adobe he found Bonnard was sitting in a plush red leather chair —part of a suite—reading. A fire crackled in the stone hearth. Though Starret guessed the camp here was very temporary, the *casa* wasn't, he decided. And it was completely in character to find Bonnard relaxed in such an expensive seat. He exuded the confidence of a rich man, and clearly had the tastes of one.

As soon as he was inside, and the door closed behind him, the Frenchman got up, motioned with a wave of his arm to the fine settee, matching the chair. Seeing it, Starret could well imagine Catalina draped across it, oozing every last drop of the feminine charms she had. As he sat down, Bonnard crossed the room to a table on which were various bottles. He poured two drinks, returned offering him one.

Starret took it and tasted it. It was fine liquor. As if reading his thoughts Bonnard said, 'From France. The brandy, I believe, favoured by Napoleon himself.'

'That should mean somethin'',' Starret said.

Bonnard raised his brows. 'It is among the finest of French brandies.' A brief smile ghosted his lips. 'You are not a connoisseur of fine liquors, Starret, I take it.'

Starret shook his head. 'I guess not, though I like a good Kentucky bourbon if I can get my hands on one. But I ain't here for that, am I?'

Again Bonnard's look was quick, sharp—similar to what it had been after he had killed Pheasy and Starret had asked why.

'No,' he said. 'You are here to help in shipping a hundred of the latest Winchesters to Geronimo, complete with ammunition.'

Starret blinked at that one, felt his gut tighten. One hundred repeating rifles to that murdering renegade...? God Almighty. Even a damned Frenchman and follower of Quantrill should know better than that.

'One hundred repeaters to that devil?' he felt compelled to repeat. 'I gotta ask you why, apart from expressing the stupidity

84

of it, any which way you look at it. For, if nothing else, no matter how big the shipment, there can't be enough real profit for you—the successful businessman you already are. Injuns just ain't got that kind of money. And I don't even need to mention the murder and mayhem that'll stem from them acquiring such weapons.'

Bonnard shrugged and a thoughtful frown clouded his brow for a moment. He said, 'Yes, maybe that is regrettable.' Then he smiled indulgently, sipped brandy appreciatively before he replied, 'But I trade not for money, Starret. No. Gold, yes.'

At that Starret felt his ears prick up, almost physically, immediate disbelief filling him. 'Gold?' he said. 'From an Apache?' He made a disparaging noise. 'From what I know, Apaches ain't acquired the habit of dealin' in the yellow metal yet. Don't mean a lot to them. They'd rather raid and steal and kill to live.'

Bonnard smiled faintly. 'Like a lot of your countrymen, you appear to have a very low opinion of the native American, Starret.'

'It ain't a low opinion,' countered Starret. 'I just can't cotton to the way they do things sometimes.'

Bonnard smiled. 'Yes, well, we could discuss that one for hours,' he said. He waved a dismissive arm. 'No matter.'

Now his eyes gleamed with greed in the pale light of the three lamps around the room as he leaned forward in his chair. 'For the facts I am dealing with are these, Starret,' he said. 'There is enough of the "yellow metal" as you call it in this transaction to make your dreams, my dreams—and all the men in this canyon's wildest dreams come true. A mine with seams as thick as your arm.'

A feeling of scornful contempt crept into Starret. He couldn't help it. 'A *mine?* You believe it?' Starret laughed derisively. 'Is that what Geronimo's been promisin'?'

Bonnard narrowed his eyelids and frowned. Anger tinged his amber stare. 'You doubt the possibility?'

Starret nodded vigorously. 'I sure as hell do,' he said. 'Damn it, he ain't the first Injun, or Mex, or American for that matter, to talk of lost mines an' fabulous wealth. Don't you know that? And if that red devil thinks he's goin' to get a hundred new repeating Winchesters out of it, he'll explain the moon is green cheese, too...'

Starret saw the faint anger Bonnard

86

had shown a couple of seconds ago fade. He seemed to accept his scathing scepticism with a cultured indulgence—like a man supremely confident that he, unlike everyone else, had found El Dorado.

'You ever heard of the Lost Vargos Mine, Starret?' he said patiently.

Starret looked into Bonnard's searching, enquiring gaze. Who hadn't? he thought. But, by God, does the man believe it?

'I've heard of the Lost Dutchman,' he said.

'You haven't answered my question,' Bonnard said. 'This is not about the Lost Dutchman. I find it difficult to believe that one myself'

Starret shook his head. He said soberly, 'Neither should you believe in any other, Bonnard. This talk of lost mines is loony longings from men full of gold fever; men who have spent too many years in the desert; too many years chasin' fool's gold and lost Spanish mines that never existed; men who have swallowed wild stories from Mexican *picaros* [cheats], who have backed up their fervent assurances with dirty, old-lookin' maps—the only genuine maps existing, they avow—and yours for a few pesos...'

Bonnard waved an arm dismissively. 'Yes, yes, I know there are such people and who but a fool would believe them?' he said excitedly. 'But this isn't a Mexican *peon*'s map, nor is it a wild claim from a sun-affected prospector. No. This is Chiricahua folk memory, handed down. This is real, I tell you. Even the history rings true. Victor Vargos was a Hungarian mercenary who came out here in the seventeenth century clutching land grants from the Spanish crown as a reward for outstanding military service in Europe on behalf of that dynasty. Exploring them he came up into the Chiricahua country—to seek his own El Dorado, I suppose, and found the gold deposits.'

Bonnard sipped brandy, his eyes shining. 'Well,' he went on, 'for trinkets dangled alluringly before them, the Chiricahua of those days helped Victor Vargos mine the gold, then watched him depart—standing alongside the holy father and his followers Vargos had left behind to build a church there and bring the true faith to the native and establish his own authority as well. But once in the desert, though, the Chiricahua—curious about the strange men—killed them all for the possession of their horses, fancy swords and armour, thinking they—their armour and horses—to have had magic powers.'

'It's a damned fairy-tale,' burst out Starret, 'unlike the Lost Dutchman, which has some credence.'

However, Starret could see there would be no turning Bonnard. Lust for such vast, promised riches blazed in his eyes. Like so many before him, Bonnard had swallowed the bait.

'But,' Bonnard went on eagerly, clearly wishing to argue down his doubt, 'you must know the history of the discovery that led to the speculation about the lost mine? Vargos's body found in the desert years later, along with his expedition of fifty men, their bones white in the sun. And those fifteen wagons with the column were full of the highest grade ore. They had been left untouched, standing there all that time, their timbers drying and warping in the hot desert winds.' Bonnard bent forward excitedly. 'Think of it, Starret, for God's sake: *fifteen wagon loads*. Can you imagine it? Where did it come from? It had to come from somewhere—'

'An' Geronimo knows where, huh?' Starret interrupted. He laughed heartily.

He couldn't help himself. 'Well, I got to give it to the red sonofabitch—it's a new one.'

Sobering after that observation, Starret held out his hands imploringly. He knew that once a man got this sort of fever through his veins it was almost impossible to quench it. However, he had to play every card he could think of to convince the Frenchman of the myth, even if it was only to ensure Geronimo did not get the Winchesters.

'Bonnard,' he said, 'the Lost Vargos Mine was given up for exactly that—*lost*—a hundred years ago. It's a myth. Forget it. Forget the guns.'

Bonnard's face altered, became slightly suspicious. And the tone in his voice betrayed his feelings. 'It is a pity,' he said, 'that you do not believe the story. And what is it to you if Geronimo gets guns or not—being the renegade you claim to be, particularly if there is gold in it—vast amounts of gold?'

'Gun-runnin' to Injuns ain't in my book,' snapped Starret. 'Hell, have you thought what Geronimo can do to the people in this territory if he does get the guns? And to maybe me and you an' this whole

90

operation? Man, we still got to operate in the territory. Don't forget that.'

Bonnard's stare had now become searching—cold and unsure. He said, 'I have found, after long experience in such matters, a desperado with scruples is not a good combination, *mon ami*. I do not like your attitude. It should not matter to you where, or to whom, the guns go.'

Starret grunted irritably. 'Well, damn it, like it or not, it does.'

Bonnard remained icy. 'Then you must realize I cannot allow you to leave us alive if you remain of this opinion?' he said, his tone completely altered and hostile. 'I must have one hundred per cent allegiance to whatever I undertake. And I cannot allow such information you now have to be made public. Do you understand?'

Starret found, even though he knew that, his throat had still gone almost completely dry. Of course, he had known from the start that Bonnard would have no scruples about killing him if he felt he had to. He had learned that for sure since being spared at the prison van. Bonnard you don't trifle with. What he says he'll do, he does. And, above all else, decided Starret, he had to stay alive to thwart him.

'Let's get one thing straight, Bonnard,' he said, not capitulating too quickly. 'I don't take kindly to threats, even bein' in the situation I am.' He shrugged. 'But if you're *convinced* Geronimo's story is genuine, well a man'd be a damned fool not to toe the line for the money to be gained out of that one.'

However, when he saw Bonnard was not wholly convinced after his stand, Starret decided he had to gamble. He went on, 'You said you liked a man to tell you the truth about how he feels.' He shrugged. 'OK. So I'll put it on the line: I don't believe in the Lost Vargos Mine, never have. But I'll be glad to be corrected on that. And in that I'm no different to most other men when the potential riches prove a reality. But what I want to know—if you do find the mine—is what goes on from there? Do I get a cut, or do I die? And what happens to the other men here? They know Louis Bonnard is behind the gun runnin'. They die too?'

Bonnard narrowed thick eyelids across piercing eyes for a moment, then nodded. A new, respectful light was in his eyes. 'Well, you're frank,' he said. 'And I thank you for it. As to your final question I'll accord you the courtesy of being frank with you in return. The other men, the twenty border scum I am employing, well...I have yet to make the decision on them. But concerning you: I do not know enough about you. Bell, James and Vigo will profit from it, they know that, for they believe in me and we have connections going back to the war. But you...no, no decision yet. You have yet to prove your complete dedication to me and my operations.'

'Bell, James, Vigo, they could have been livin' a lie,' Starret pointed out. 'Who's to say they won't kill you soon as they know about the mine, claim it for themselves?'

Bonnard nodded. 'It is an interesting point. But we have been together a long time. I know those men. They are honourable with me, as I am with them. I am not afraid of what you suggest.'

'And Pheasy...?'

Regret flashed across Bonnard's amber eyes for a moment then he said, 'It was a pity about Pheasy, for I trusted him. But he broke the rules I laid down years ago and he paid the price.' Warning darkened his look. 'Don't you, Starret...don't you break the rules.'

Noting the threat, Starret finished his brandy. 'And the border trash?'

Bonnard's stare became void of expression. He made a nervous pull at one of the buttons on the red leather of the chair. 'I have several plans,' he said.

But Starret could tell by Bonnard's attitude that the discussion was now to be wrapped up. He said, 'So that's it, huh?'

Bonnard nodded. 'That's it,' he said. 'Be ready to leave for Mexico in half an hour.'

'The guns are there?' Starret said.

Bonnard paused as if momentarily undecided, then nodded again and poured himself more brandy. 'Yes.' But that was all he appeared prepared to say. 'Now, find and send Catalina to me, will you?'

'Sure,' Starret said.

He went out into the night gut-taut, the charade he had played out in there making him cold-scared in the knowledge that Geronimo was more than likely to get his hands on this big shipment of repeating Winchesters. The very notion of it didn't bear thinking about. And he felt completely impotent concerning

94

it, enough to have indecision gnawing at him with unfamiliar ferocity. How was he to get word out?

He shook his head. And how to handle it best? That was the problem. He had to let Bonnard get his guns. The possibility, then, of Geronimo getting his hands on them depended on the actual existence of the Lost Vargos Mine. He felt sure Bonnard would want solid visual proof of the actuality of that baby before even considering handing over the boxes the rifles were maybe in. The whole deal must surely hinge on that.

And the confirmation of that had yet to be. Maybe when Bonnard returned from Mexico with the guns, Geronimo would spring his own trap and just take them, having duped Bonnard into putting up the money and Soam setting up the deal. The whole story about the Lost Vargos Mine was maybe just Geronimo's tasty appetizer, deliberately devised knowing the white man's driving lust for gold.

He narrowed his eyes as he stared at the quarter moon rising above the canyon rimrock. It was going to be one hell of a journey to Mexico—and an even more interesting one when they returned.

SIX

The trip through the desert country proved to be five days of burning hell. So it was with deep relief Starret climbed with Bonnard's hard-bitten crew, up into the relatively cooler air of the Mexican sierras—well south of the border.

Catalina had come with them, unlike the other women, who had stayed behind in the canyon, which made sense to Starret, for he considered this no trip for females; but, he found, to his mild surprise, Catalina seemed to endure the desert trip better than most.

And, more surprising, considering the first welcome he had received from her to Bonnard's owlhoot nest, she had hardly spoken to, or come near to him, the whole journey, which puzzled him slightly. Maybe Bonnard had called enough... If so, he was thankful for that. He didn't want any unnecessary entanglements, for Catalina was a powerfully tempting woman to have hanging around you.

He took his thoughts away from her to review the ride here. On the first day into the desert they had seen little that was living to bother them—apart from the natural population of gila monsters, lizards and so on. But on the second day a party identified as Lipan Apaches had crested a long escarpment to the right of the trail they rode and gazed at them, staying well out of rifle range.

After these hardened desert dwellers had given them a long and leisurely examination they disappeared into the merciless expanse of rocky, cactus-studded desolation once more. And the savage heat —forgotten during those tense moments— had returned again to plague Starret.

But the encounter had stuck in his mind. Maybe the Indians had decided Bonnard's party was too big to tackle; nearly thirty men, armed to the teeth. From the start it had been clear to Starret, Bonnard was not intending to take any chances. And any opportunist Mexican *bandidos* they encountered would, Starret reckoned, with understandable discretion, think twice before tackling this column. Ruminating even more while he rode, Starret considered maybe all these men would also encourage Geronimo to fulfil the promise he'd made of revealing the Lost Vargos Mine in exchange for rifles. A party as large as this would certainly dissuade the Apache renegade away from maybe forgetting the agreements entered into and just taking the rifles; or would it...?

Starret thinned his lips. Maybe...but it was clear, by the sure way Bonnard picked his trail across the desert, that the Frenchman had been here before and knew exactly where he was going. He rode the trail with complete assurance, erect in his long duster coat and fancy stetson, eating fine meals in the evening with Catalina, and consulting a compass only occasionally.

So late morning of this fifth day found them descending deep into a narrow canyon, and becoming uncomfortable under the relentless heat of the hot sun as it closed in on them.

In the bottom, Starret found a trickle of water traced a leaden path through it until, journeying west, they came to a cascade of water which virtually sprang out of the barren rock to form a deep pool of clear water on the floor of the canyon. There was lush grass here, too—and shade from the trees around the pool.

An hour after sating his thirst and relaxing in this glorious oasis with the other members of the party, Starret was completely unready for the group of fifteen men dressed as *Rurales* and surrounding two wagons who appeared from around the bend a half-mile south, down the canyon.

And seeing them he tightened his grip on the Winchester in his hand. He decided immediately that this could be nasty—near thirty Americans, armed to the teeth, deep in Mexico? And it should prove interesting as to how Bonnard was going to handle it.

But seeing them Starret was surprised to see the Frenchman spur forward with Catalina at his side, sitting her beautiful palomino mare with the easy assurance of a woman used to the saddle.

The column of *Rurales*—if that was what they were—came to a stop. Reaching them Starret saw Bonnard shake hands warmly with the lieutenant leading the line of men and soon Catalina was interpreting the talk.

Starret narrowed his eyes. So that was

what she was here for... He spat, wiped his sweat-damp brow. He should have realized it.

After some talk Bonnard reached behind him, into his saddle-bags. He lifted out what appeared to be two heavy sacks. He handed them over to the lieutenant, who hefted them. And feeling the weight and hearing the chink, his white teeth below the pencil-thin moustache decorating his upper lip, flashed against his dark skin. He opened them and checked the contents. Then, as if signalling his satisfaction as to their contents, his smile broadened into a grin.

The officer was about to put them into his own saddle-bags when Bonnard shook his head and waggled his finger. The lieutenant lost his smile and his face darkened with resentment. There was more talk, heated this time, Catalina giving it full animation in the interpretation, then the *Rurale* officer bobbed his head as if, finally, though reluctant to agree to Bonnard's wishes, he would hand back the bags. Having done so he waved a brisk, condescending hand to Bonnard to accompany him to the first of the wagons.

Starret watched impassively while Bonnard had every long box out of the first wagon opened. As if randomly, he selected several rifles and inspected them thoroughly before replacing them. Starret could see they were clearly new—still greased and wrapped in oilpaper.

As if satisfied, Bonnard nodded briskly, waved and watched as the boxes of ammunition now came out. They, too, were scrutinized meticulously.

Then the empty wagon driven from the American side was drawn up alongside and loaded with the rifles and ammunition. After it was all completed to Bonnard's satisfaction, the bags were passed over once more. American eagles or Mexican pesos? It mattered little, decided Starret. Either way the guns were real, the money was real. Clearly, a long-planned deal had been completed to mutual satisfaction.

Without any further fraternization between the two parties, they parted. The rattle of the hooves of the *Rurales'* horses clattered away into silence down the canyon and out of sight.

When they'd gone Bonnard turned, a beaming grin on his face as he surveyed the large party under the trees.

'OK, men,' he said. 'Let's head for home.'

On the trail out of the canyon, though, Starret was surprised when Bonnard drew his fine black mare alongside him. 'What do you think now, my doubting friend?' he demanded.

Starret smiled thinly, shrugged. 'Fine...so far, I guess.'

Bonnard waved his arm triumphantly. 'Fine? The transaction was perfect. Not a hitch. Do not be so pessimistic.'

Starret nodded. His cautious nature, nurtured by more than one disappointment in life and the hope that this transaction would not take place, anyway—and not helped by the perilous situation he was now in—permitted him only to say, 'If you say so, Bonnard.'

But it was the consequences of the trade that depressed Starret most, but naturally, he could not reveal that. He would have to wait until they got back to Arizona, then...

Starret looked grimly at the shimmering ochre-coloured desert before him. Visions of warpainted Apaches thundering down on settlements brandishing brand new Winchesters haunted him for a moment, but only a moment. He was a man who usually lived for the day. Tomorrow would take care of itself, if he gave it a little help.

And he had to do that.

SEVEN

Night found Starret camped with Bonnard's party ten miles from the canyon meet point with the corrupt *Rurales*—if that was what they were. He wasn't sure. The camp was buzzing with optimism and clearly without scruples about the business.

Starret looked over his plate of fatback, coffee and beans. Across the campfire, Joe Bell grinned at him.

'Whut you think of Bonnard now, Morgan?' he said.

Starret shrugged. 'Well, he ain't a fool, that's for sure.'

Joe raised grey-streaked eyebrows and stared at him. 'Hell, we're on our way!' he crowed. 'Whut about all thet gold when Geronimo comes over with the mine?'

'If he comes over,' Starret said.

He could see John Rigo and Clute James were staring at him, too, but, he thought, for different reasons. He still had the strong feeling that he had not yet been forgiven for thrashing Pheasy back in the canyon hideout, or forgiven for the outcome of that triumph—Pheasy's death. But they didn't blame Bonnard for shooting him, he decided. No. Pheasy had broken the rules. But he, Starret, a stranger, had caused Pheasy to break those rules...and that was something else.

Starret growled impatiently at his over-active conjectures into other people's thinking. He didn't know what they thought. That was the truth of it.

'Hell,' grunted Joe Bell butting in on his silent speculations, 'but you're a pessimistic cuss, Morgan. Ain't you moved at all about the deal?'

'Not 'til it happens,' Starret said.

Rigo said, as if he, too, was puzzled, 'Half of it has happened. Ain't you been let in on the Vargos mine deal yet?'

Starret nodded. 'Sure. If the mine exists.'

Rigo made an optimistic noise and spat. 'Hell, it's there all right,' he said confidently. 'You kin bet real money on thet. Bonnard has a nose for a deal—keen as a hound dog's.'

A coyote yipped, out in the night. Starret turned towards the direction of it, his ears straining. Another call came in answer. Bell, Rigo and James, too, had gone silent and attentive.

After moments Bell wiped his mouth put down his tin plate and said, 'Whut you think, Morgan?'

Starret shook his head, the grim contours of his face etched in the light from the small fire they sat around. 'Don't know,' he admitted. 'Just don't know. Could be Apache.'

Rigo spat, looked doubtful. 'Maybe not, too. Them Lipans have had a view of us. They know our strength. Ain't enough of them to bother us, what I saw.'

'Could have gotten reinforcements,' countered James, his slightly bulging eyes round and active in their sockets. 'This is maybe another bunch altogether—nothin' to do with them.'

Bell nodded enthusiastically. 'Yeah, thet's how I feel.'

Vigo said, 'You think they're in with the *Rurales?*'

James glared. 'You crazy?' he said. 'The

Mexes just purely hate the Apache. Mebbe more'n us even.'

''Tain't unknown,' Joe said. 'I heard onct—'

A long scream rent the night, cutting off any other conversation. It was female. Then Starret detected a scuffle was going on over where he knew Catalina had been sitting staring out at the desert and the stars.

Staccato gunfire came from the right of them now and Vigo cried out harshly as he fell into the fire. He rolled out again moaning, a part of his greasy clothes smouldering.

With Joe Bell and Clute James, Starret exploded away from the firelight, gun out, leaving Vigo to crawl into the bushes nearby while attempting to brush off the tiny flames on his coat. He was clearly in pain, too.

More shots rang out. Lead began fizzing with deadly noise through the night. Now, all around him, Starret realized the camp was in uproar. Shouts and the harsh noise of gunfire began rippling into the desert stillness, stabbing the growing darkness with spiteful flame as campfires started to be stamped out.

But that had been Catalina screaming, Starret realized. Gathering himself from his initial alarm, he was now certain sure of that. And with the knowledge he felt a deep anxiety growing in him. His gut tightened. For God's sake, not Catalina. He reckoned she was just an innocent pawn in this deadly game and he'd seen what Apaches could do to women.

On impulse he got to his feet and bounded over on long legs to where he knew the Mexican temptress had been. Nothing, just the beautiful silk wrap she had had draped around her shoulders, lying on the ground.

Now he heard Bonnard shouting orders. 'Take cover...hold your positions...make sure of your target...do not leave the perimeter...' A military man, for sure, Starret decided grimly. And, he thought hotly, he clearly had no thoughts for Catalina.

The vicious barrage of fire that had come from the desert with such startling suddenness moments ago following Catalina's cry, began to subside until the shooting became desultory then faded altogether. A nervous, waiting watchfulness descended over the camp.

Starret went after Bonnard and found him by the wagon with the rifles and ammunition in it. He was with ten other men, all in its cover. For sure, Starret thought disgustedly when he saw it, the arms wagon, choose what happened to Catalina, was going to remain in Bonnard's hands.

'Your woman has been taken,' he rasped, still clutching his hand gun and glaring through the dark at the Frenchman.

Bonnard looked unmoved. His only reaction was to take a fresh grip on his fancy Smith & Wesson. 'Catalina knows she'll have to take her chances—like the rest of us,' he said.

Starret stared. 'Take her chances? Damn it—'

Bonnard's amber stare was fierce as it met his own. 'What do you expect me to do, Starret?' he demanded, cutting in. 'Ride out there after her?'

The reply from Starret burst anxiously from his lips; no thought behind it. 'For God's sake—somethin' like that,' he rasped.

Bonnard's look was now steady, searching. 'Such gallantry,' he said, after moments. 'But, calm down, man, and think. They have not killed her, or you would have found her dead. So perhaps they want something. Perhaps a trade of some sort. We will remain vigilant for the night, then see what the dawn brings. OK?'

Starret felt he was almost trembling with the passion and fear that was in him. 'OK?' he barked. 'What the hell you mean? OK. Hell's bells, they'll rape her, then kill her, that's what the Apache'll do. Damn it, don't you know?'

What served for blood in Bonnard's veins? Starret found himself thinking angrily. Ice? Damn it, this was the man's woman he was talking about. A warm, generous woman whom he could easily love himself. He felt rage now burning in the pit of his stomach.

'Bonnard—' he started.

'You stay in camp, Starret,' Bonnard warned, cutting abruptly across his words. 'That is an order. OK?'

Starret found invective against Bonnard rising into his gorge. 'To hell with your OK!' he raged. He turned, swallowing his anger, and went off into the night to find cover.

'No heroics, Starret,' Bonnard called out after him.

But all Starret could see was Catalina's flashing smile, her green alluring eyes, her lovely Titian hair. All he could feel was the vibrant vivacity that had oozed out of her as she had teased him in the canyon that night—alive and generous. This was no way for a woman of her vitality to go, by God it wasn't. He had to do something.

He waited for the camp to go still again. Fires were stoked up to give light to the perimeter, but with men placed well out of their reaching light. He could see Bonnard had set up a trap, too—a killing ground of crossfire. It was a grand plan, in textbook style, but Apaches were seldom that accommodating.

An hour later Starret reached Pheasy's pinto undetected, saddled him and went into the desert night.

The only plan he had was to find Catalina, then...

Who knows? Starret knew he had to play this one by ear.

EIGHT

By sun up Starret was lying on a high ochre-coloured bluff, the pinto tied up in the cover of rocks below the skyline behind him. He gazed keenly across the rocky, broken desert. Saguaros stood like giant sentinels, gold in the dawn. Between the rocky spaces, the dark, wasteland green of cholla and creosote brush was washed pale by the sun sitting like a huge golden orb on the distant, blue-veined horizon.

He had seen the Indian campfires last night. They must be feeling damned confident of their position, he thought moodily as he stared. And now, in the light of the new day, he observed, as he expected it would be, that it was a temporary camp of hastily made *jacals* looking like rough, upturned birds' nests amid the rocks on a stretch of rising ground below him. It was clearly a bronco camp. He could see no squaws.

Through a small telescope he had found in Soam's things he searched the camp

111

thoroughly. After a brief scan he found what he was looking for—Catalina's sun-brightened bronze hair, shining like a beacon amongst the dark wiry locks of the Apaches.

She was sitting on her own, her knees hunched up against her once-white blouse, arms around her legs, which were wrapped in her long green skirt. From what he could see—the weak magnification of the glass barely sufficient for the distance—she was unharmed.

Thank God for that, he thought with relief.

Too, there was much activity down there. Braves were streaking on warpaint, tending to rifles, eating, preparing horses.

When the sun finally stood on its own in the sky—clear of the horizon—Catalina was grabbed roughly and dragged to her feet. Her protesting screams came very faintly to his ears through the still air, and his hand tightened instinctively on his Winchester at the sound of it.

Then he saw her pushed towards a small buckskin pony and forced astride it, a rawhide thong placed around her neck and made tight enough to cause her clear discomfort, but not enough to garrotte her, unless she tried to break away. To Starret, it appeared to be a hellish device, but only what he knew he could expect from the Apache.

Now the Lipan party—fierce of visage and purposeful—rode out towards Bonnard's camp. Seeing the site in the far distance, Starret had noted earlier the Frenchman had picked its position well—on rising ground—elevating it above the scattered flora of the desert floor. And Starret could see thin columns of blue smoke were rising from it, men around them cooking. He narrowed eyelids webbed with faint crow's-feet at the corners and spat. Seemed, even though Catalina could have been suffering all manner of torments, breakfast was not to be forgotten.

He scrambled down to his own mount cropping at a patch of teosinte grass it had found and climbed up. Astride, he eased it down the gentler slope of the bluff, keeping in the cover of the broken ground around it.

And, not at all aware of the grim manoeuvres going on, the desert was alive with fluting song-birds flitting gleam-feathered in the golden sunshine, busy amongst the tall cacti. It would have been an uplifting scene, had it not been for the deadly activities being played out.

Now on the desert floor, and with the help of a long arroyo, he edged his way to where the Apaches had eased up and were now staring at Bonnard's camp. After moments of intense study on the Apaches' part Starret watched a brave edge his mount out into the open—a white rag tied and lying limp against his ancient Sharp's rifle. He waved it above his head.

Having been signalled by the camp to come on in he moved, slapping Catalina's buckskin pony into motion along with his own. With his other hand the brave tugged at the thong around her neck viciously, a grin of cruel delight on his swarthy face.

Starret was close enough to hear Catalina cry out before she made choking noises. She leaned towards the buck to lessen the cutting effect of the rawhide around her neck and urged the buckskin on to catch up.

Assessing his situation quickly Starret judged himself to be about 150 yards from the scene he watched, still in good cover because of the depth and curve of the dry river bed he had found and followed. And all the time he was feverishly calculating his chances of getting Catalina free.

With a hell of a lot of luck riding with him, he decided, he could maybe charge out, snatch Catalina and reach Bonnard's camp unscathed—the surprise rendering the Apaches impotent for those first few vital seconds he would need.

He licked his dry lips. That had to be the plan if all else failed—if Bonnard didn't come through with something, that is. For the plain fact was, nobody yet knew what the Lipans were wanting.

A hundred yards from Bonnard's camp a rifle was abruptly fired into the air. Immediately the brave stopped as if alarmed by it, then tugged viciously at the rawhide thong around Catalina's neck so that she was drawn close to him. Then Starret heard him rap fast talk to her in Spanish.

After he had slackened the thong, Catalina shouted, 'Louis, they want thee guns from you een exchange for me. Eef you love me, do eet. Plis, oh, plis. They weel keel me eef you don't.'

Bonnard's reply came back with a cheerfulness that sent anger scurrying hotly through Starret. 'You knew perhaps that this would happen, *mon amour,*' he said.

'But take heart, *cherie*. They are bluffing, I am sure. We will think of something to free you never fear. Stay calm.'

'No! No! Louis!' Catalina's return cry was laden with fear and desperation. 'They are not bluffing!'

The anguish in the plea cut into Starret like an Apache war blade. In an odd and unwanted way, he had grown fond of the woman. She had a vitality, an aliveness he found to be almost intoxicating, despite her connections with Bonnard.

And it caused him to glare from his cover at the Frenchman's camp. Damn you, Bonnard, he thought bitterly. What's a few damned rifles!

But he found he had to withdraw the thought immediately it came to him. For, he knew, the possession of the rifles could be a lot of things. It did not matter that the rifles were in Geronimo's hands or these Lipan Apaches—far from their west Texas homeland—the end result would be the same: rampaging death and destruction throughout the south-west, maybe for years to come.

He swallowed hard and blinked. One life—even Catalina's—against that?

Appalled and feeling diminished by the

dilemma, Starret brought a trembling hand up to his stubbled chin. For most men, it would be an awesome decision to make. Not, though, for Bonnard, it seemed.

He narrowed his eyelids as his instincts about such men came to the fore. He had little doubt what would be Bonnard's reaction to this predicament. Catalina would be no contest in the high stakes the Frenchman was playing for. Starret had already witnessed the cold ruthlessness of the man that, he guessed, no love would thaw where the riches to be gained from the forthcoming transaction with Geronimo was concerned. Starret assumed the Frenchman's view would be that Catalina had been a pleasant diversion, but now the dice had fallen bad for her she must be served up on the altar of necessity.

Starret watched as the brave again tugged at the rawhide thong. Its vicious snatch was enough to cause Catalina to cry out once more. Then the Apache spoke again and she started sobbing, her courage clearly fading as she began to realize that a terrible death could be a possibility.

She turned to the camp, her face crumpled with anxiety, her green eyes made round with her anguish. 'Louis!' she bawled. *'Madre de Dios!* Plis do as they want! Oh, plis! Eef you love me. For *I* love you so much!'

The plea made, the Apache slid off his horse and dragged Catalina to the ground with him. With his war axe he drove a long stake into the rocky soil, tied her hands behind her and fastened the thong around her neck securely to the stake. Then he stood up grinning at the camp and shaking his rifle.

Seeing it, rage crawled through Starret's gut and he glared at the scene being enacted.

His demonstration made, the Apache turned lithely and jumped on to his pony's back and turned to head towards the others. But Starret wasn't ready for the single, booming shot from the perimeter of Bonnard's fortification. The brave was knocked clean off his horse. His cry of pain was stark as he sprawled into the desert dust to flop about like a banked fish before stiffening out. Birds, disturbed by the noise, flew squawking into the brassy day.

Starret blinked lids over cold eyes. He knew that rifle. It was the big buffalo-killing Sharps, owned by Joe Bell—the one that had cut down Deputy US Marshal John Hayes and the prison van driver, Charlie.

And as soon as the killing happened, Starret stiffened and felt dreadful alarm surge through him—enough to prickle up his hair ends and crawl across his scalp. Damn Bell to hell! he silently raged. That was going to cause all sorts of mayhem to start rolling here. And Catalina was right in the middle of it.

But somehow, he didn't think it was done of Joe's own volition. Bonnard's hand must have been behind it. The Frenchman, despite what it would cost Catalina, was making it plain where the Apaches stood with him. If they wanted the guns, they were going to have to come and take them—over Catalina's dead body if need be.

Angry whoops came from the group of Lipans. A volley from old singleshots rattled the desert morning with snarling violence. But, to Starret's relief, Catalina did not go down. When the volley died down she was still standing there, quivering with fright.

Starret's gaze hardened. It was an old Apache ploy, staking Catalina out like this. These hardened people had acquired the same cruel, but neutral nature of the desert they roamed; the same concept of time even, the same attitude to the inevitability of the destiny of all things—be the recipients of that destiny, man or beast. They had, like the desert—patience; patience to attain what they desired. For life and time was ever turning—endless. Inevitably, the balance would be tilted in their favour, if they waited long enough, and the sun got to work on Catalina.

It was the wearing down effect on the susceptible mind, or the cat playing with the mouse, or the probing of your adversary's strength, or weakness. Yes, the Apache could wait. They did not have clocks to stare worriedly at. The White Eyes had invented *them*. All the Apache had was the sun and the moon and the seasons. The four points of the world. And the earth, the sky.

So they could wait—wait while the more sensitive members of Bonnard's camp witnessed Catalina die in slow agony from thirst, under the blazing sun of the desert; wait while they listened to her terrible pleas as they faded and diminished with her life.

Maybe, the Apaches would be thinking in their stoic way, her whimpers and cries would test how hard and strong the White Eye's heart and mind really was when it was so sorely tried. Was it as strong as an Apache's? Would the sensitive of the camp prevail over the strong in demanding Catalina's release from her torment...?

Starret blinked. He reckoned Bonnard would have no problem with Catalina's martyrdom, but *he* had. Starret's gut knotted. He'd never had to face a dilemma like this before. And he was a man who liked to act, when action was needed. And he had a heart, too, that could be moved...as it was being moved now, tormented even.

Catalina was standing moaning, her head bowed, her lovely Titian hair draped about her classic features, hiding them. God almighty, when the sun really started to get to her...

Starret narrowed his eyelids once more across his grey eyes. He lifted his strong chin. Well, the one thing the Apaches had overlooked was the White Eyes, for the most part, like himself, were not stoics. They had this occasional unpredictability and rash impulsiveness that made them do

121

crazy, irrational things.

Like right now.

He drew the long knife he had found in Soam's effects, and kicked Pheasy's pinto into surging life. From the moment he began to ride it the horse had proved itself to be a surefooted, lively cuss with great stamina that relished a fast run over rough ground. But, Starret knew, too, in the next few moments, its qualities would never be more crucially tested. That was for sure.

Within seconds he had covered the distance between the arroyo and Catalina and was slashing apart the rawhide thong holding her. Then, his teeth gritted, he was hoisting her across the pinto's withers before the Apache realized what was happening. And, realizing he was getting away with it, Starret emitted a long, wild 'Yeeeeehaaaah!' as he dug his boots in for the final run for the camp.

And he found he was surging with an incredible elation as he ran, his blood roaring through him. It came almost as a relief when rifle fire began to splutter up from behind him and from the camp in front of him. Though any moment he expected lead to thump into him it didn't and he was thundering into Bonnard's camp within twenty seconds of erupting from the arroyo.

Tingling with elation he dropped off the pinto and brought Catalina down with him. Before he could do anything about it—not that he wanted to, he realized abruptly—Catalina was in his arms.

'Oh! Morgan Starret!' she was enthusing. 'My *mucho* gringo bull! Thees time you are thee great matador!'

Starret felt her kisses smacking all over his unwashed and unshaven face as she clung to him, her tears of relief moistening his own face as well as her own.

Reluctantly he eased her off him. 'Now hold on, Catalina,' he protested with a grin. 'I only saved your life, maybe!'

Catalina's own appreciative laugh was throaty and abandoned as it bubbled from her, the tension she had been living with for the past hours with the Apache now clearly released.

'*Si*,' she said, 'all thee time—you Americanos can make thee joke about eet, but for Catalina, eet ees not a joke. Eet ees love for the *mucho hombre* who has come into Catalina's life!'

Starret found he was undecided about

wanting to hear that—for there was still Bonnard to keep on the good side of, and there was still the rifles, and there was still the need to stop Geronimo getting his hands on them, and there was also Catalina's own fickle unpredictability.

'Yeah, well maybe when you've cooled off a little, Catalina,' he said, easing her off him. 'You'll maybe see it a little different.'

Drowning any more words, more rifle fire rang out from the desert and the thrum of hooves running over hard ground came, and the war whoops of the frustrated Apache.

Starret could hear Bonnard shouting, 'Keep your positions! Fire on my command!'

As the first hum of lead passed him, Starret pulled Catalina against one of the wagons. Then he handed her his sixgun.

'Get under there,' he ordered. 'Behind the wheel. Stay low and stay there. And use the gun if you have to.'

He then got up and snatched his rifle from its saddle scabbard and tied his nervous pinto to the tail gate of the wagon Catalina was under.

When he faced the desert again he could

see the Apaches were firing their rifles and running their mounts freely around the camp perimeter, fortified by Bonnard's military mind and in a commanding position on this low knoll. When Bonnard had picked this spot last night, Starret realized, he knew exactly what he was doing and had anticipated an attack. He had the precise, military mind, that took few chances.

'Fire at will!' came Bonnard's command.

The splutter of gunfire roared out from the perimeter—twenty-five guns in a devastating volley. Starret watched as the barrage decimated the Apache ranks. It was brutal, organized slaughter.

Now, Starret heard the gunfire from the perimeter become spattering and disorganised, but none the less deadly for that, for he knew the men behind the guns were long practised in their use.

Reaching the edge of the fortifications, Starret dived into a shallow trench clearly dug out during the night and brought his Winchester into play, but already he saw the Apaches seemed to have lost the stomach for it. He knew they had neither the weapons, nor the numbers to match the camp's defences. And he knew they knew it, too.

Now he could see able braves were dragging wounded across withers or croup and riding out of range, yelling defiance at the jeers of the white men as they did. At 400 yards, out in the desert, they regrouped to count their losses.

But it wasn't over, not yet, Starret learnt swiftly. Again he heard Joe Bell's Sharps thunder out—and, even at this long range, a brave was smacked back out of the saddle to lie motionless on the desert floor. He heard the distant shouts of dismay run through the Lipan ranks. With alacrity they began to move even further away.

Again the rifle boomed; again another brave hit the desert dirt. And Starret felt grim respect begin rising in him for Bell's devastating marksmanship.

The threat of the big gun drove the Lipans way into the desert until they were out of sight. It was then Starret realized Bonnard had come up behind him.

The Frenchman stared at him with neutral eyes. He said, 'I congratulate you, Starret. It was bravely done, but it was done against orders.'

'I ain't in the army, Bonnard,' Starret

rasped. 'I figured that li'l lady needed help.'

Bonnard smiled indulgently. 'Yes, and indeed she did,' he said, 'but you have just witnessed what sound military organization can do to a rabble force when given the chance.' Starret felt Bonnard's pat on his arm. He said confidently, 'I would have secured her safety, eventually, never fear.'

Starret narrowed his eyelids, angered by Bonnard's indifference and superior attitude. 'Well, mister, you've just witnessed what independent action, *without* orders, can do, too,' he said hotly. 'And I couldn't wait that long. Why, damn it, I reckon you were prepared to let Catalina die out there. That right?'

For a moment, a look of what appeared to be heart-felt pain passed cross Bonnard's features before he gave a Gallic shrug. 'Regrettably,' he said, 'you must appreciate that, sometimes, for the greater good, harsh decisions have to be made. Catalina fully understood that. We have discussed it often enough. But as I explained, the game was far from over when you intervened. I already had a plan to reach her.'

Starret spat to the dry, already hot earth. 'Well, damn' it, you could've fooled me.'

And, as if agreeing with him, Catalina came out from under the wagon. In passing she returned Starret's gun to him, then, with a stream of Spanish invective bursting from her, she stood, her arms akimbo, her green eyes flashing, staring at Bonnard.

'I am not thee game, Louis!' she shouted.

Then, spitting and screaming like a she-cat, she went for him, her small fists flailing against his chest and arms.

But Bonnard was laughing as he took Catalina's forearms in his strong grasp and wrestled with her to disarm her assault. And, as he did so, Starret realized the Frenchman was staring at him over her head with amused eyes, a grin on his broad face.

'Have you ever seen such fire, Starret?' he demanded. 'Is it any wonder I love her. My fair Catalina is a challenge for any man, don't you think?'

After a fierce, clearly stress-releasing struggle, Starret watched Catalina sink trembling into Bonnard's arms and the Frenchman fell to stroking her tousled Titian hair and talking soothingly to her.

And it shocked Starret to see it, and bewildered him. What the hell was the woman doing? That damned Frenchman, not minutes ago, had almost condemned her to death, whether she knew the odds or not. And she did know them, he was sure of that.

He shook his head. Would he ever understand the contrariness of women? And what chance would he have with her if ever he got out of this business alive? And, damn it, why was he thinking like this? He was in enough deep water as it was, without the complication of Catalina.

He stared coldly at Bonnard and fought down his feelings for Catalina. 'When you figure to push on?' he said. 'I reckon the Lipan's phased for a spell.'

Bonnard kissed Catalina briefly before he disentangled himself from her, murmuring to her about the necessity of business first but he would, he assured, see 'mon cherie' later, never fear. Looking on, Starret guessed that the words he didn't understand were French, and something nice. He growled impatiently, maybe a little jealously.

Free of Catalina, Bonnard faced him, raising his thick eyebrows. 'Well, I think the Apache have learned their lesson,' he said confidently. 'And I think it will be safe to continue immediately. We have to rendezvous with Geronimo in three days.'

Three days? A cold feeling bit deep into Starret's bowels. He had but three days to put a stop to all this?

Attempting to ignore Catalina, though she was now staring and smiling admiringly at her 'American *toro*', he made for the chuck wagon. He'd see what the cook with the outfit had to offer, for he was ravenously hungry after his night out on the desert. And to the Alamo with Catalina's coquettishness—and her dangerous flirtatiousness. But then, he didn't really feel that either...

NINE

Late afternoon the second day Starret could see there was still dust rising way behind them. The Lipans hadn't let go yet.

Bonnard had been keeping an eye on them too, using his high-powered telescope, which, he boasted, was German made and which he had brought with him from France to use in the crazy (his words) American war in which he had been a guerrilla. And, he also seemed to want to convey to Starret, the fact that it was German meant quality.

After using it, Starret knew what he meant. The spyglass was clear and very powerful. Though they were three, four miles back, it brought the Lipans up real close. Their numbers were down from what he had seen in their camp. Some that were riding were in a bad way from wounds, too, it appeared.

But the fact that they were still there increased the uneasiness Starret was already experiencing, winding the tension he felt up another notch, which didn't help in his other troubles.

But with some slight relief, camp that night was made over the border in Arizona and Starret felt he could almost touch the sense of relaxation that descended on the owlhoots after they had crossed that magic line. For to be free of Mexico, and the possibility of meeting up with a bunch of straight *Rurales* and maybe requested to reveal the nature of their cargo—and the consequences arising from it—was one niggle that had been on the minds of all, including himself.

Even so, Starret found he couldn't relax fully. For him there was still Catalina's sometimes bold advances that could land him in trouble with Bonnard and maybe ruin his clandestine position here—and there was still the guns to Geronimo. Above everything else, he had to somehow stop them reaching that cruel-eyed Chiricahua.

Starret ate supper moodily, thinking about it. At the moment, he decided, he had about as much chance as a snowball in hell of getting free of this camp, and getting far enough away to keep his hide intact long enough to get help. At the moment, everybody was too sharp, because of the Lipans out there, waiting. And it was a short odds bet that Geronimo would maybe have scouts following the party every bend in the trail, too, though he had seen nothing to indicate it.

He had just washed his plate in a nearby stream and was stowing it in his saddle-bag when Bonnard approached him. 'You seem to know a little about the Apache, Starret,' he said. 'Do you think those out there will do anything?'

Starret wasn't in the mood to wrap

anything up, not that there was any point anyway. 'They'll give it another try. They wouldn't be following otherwise.'

Bonnard's amber eyes hardened and his chin jutted from his strong, square face. 'Then they will regret it,' he said, and moved off into the night.

Starret had noted that, yet again, the Frenchman had chosen his ground well and had a rota for defending it worked out. A four-hour stint on watch for half the camp while the others slept, then change over to the rested ones to see them through to daybreak.

The star-jewelled night that had closed down around them brought with it the Apache communication calls again; hard to detect, but clear to the knowledgeable ear. And it had stern-visaged men on watch looking keen-eyed into the darkness— licking dry lips, fingering long guns, and spitting juice nervously.

Starret had been told earlier he had been allotted a position on the northern rim of the defences. And an hour after he had settled there and the camp had gone quiet—to his surprise and irritation—Catalina sidled up to him out of the night.

It was the first time he had seen her since breaking camp that morning. All yesterday she had stayed in the wagon she and Bonnard used for sleeping and dressing in, though Bonnard had ridden with the column all day, frequently scanning the skyline, the wagon with the guns surrounded the whole time by rifle-carrying, hard-eyed men.

She plucked at his arm with slender fingers.

'For thee first time I am afraid, Morgan Starret,' she said. He could see her face was grey and drawn from her experiences with the Lipans, and her eyes were big and round. She pressed up to him. 'Geeve me some of your courage, my brave bull,' she whispered.

'Ask Bonnard for some of his,' he said shortly, though he didn't mean to be cruel. This just wasn't the time or place. 'You know damn well that's where you oughta be—with him. And, damn it, be quiet. I gotta hear good.'

'Louis can be so cold on the trail,' she went on. 'And I am wanting love—warmth.' Her big, unhappy stare found his for a moment. 'You are warm, Morgan Starret. Louis—at thee moment—he theenk more of hees gold than he does of Catalina. And he make Catalina sad because now she knows that for sure.'

She waved a limp, tired arm. 'First, I theenk—when he first say it—that Louis say thees things about taking chance on capture and not maybe geeving help eef I am. But he did mean what he say, didn't he, Morgan Starret?'

'Yes, Catalina,' Starret said. 'He meant what he said, if he said that. Now, honey, go get some sleep, huh?'

But Starret felt torn by her, unsettled. Contradicting emotions churned in him. He didn't want her here—yet he did.

He stared into the night moodily. It was still black out there. The moon had yet to rise. But they would be there, the Apache, he knew. They wanted revenge; blood in return for blood. And they wanted the guns, too, if they could get them.

A swift glance saw Catalina was pouting at him. 'I always knew eet, deep een here'—she pressed her magnificent bosom with a slim hand, near the heart, ignoring his request for her to leave—'that Louis was cold and cruel,' she said, her big eyes sadly gazing at him. 'So why do I steel love heem?'

135

Starret grunted his cynicism. 'You askin' *me?*'

She sighed. 'Ah, my matador, eet ees a different kind of love I have for *you,*' she said. 'A gentle kind of love. Not thee kind of love I have for Louis—wheech ees passion and fire.'

Starret growled, his irritation growing. This was crazy. He wasn't her damned confessor. Didn't want to be. He wanted to be her lover. And if she thought he was gentle, she'd got it wrong, too, dead wrong. But he wasn't exactly sure what she meant, which irritated him even more.

'Damn it,' he growled, 'how many kinds of love you got, woman?'

'I can love thee man who ees brave,' she said. 'That ees good. But I can also love thee man who geeves me the pretty theengs—love *heem* like crazy, sometimes—even eef he ees cruel.'

She swayed her hips with habitual provocativeness under her long skirt, but she still looked sad, a little lost—confused, maybe, Starret decided. He stared into the night, fingering his Winchester uneasily.

She was saying, her head lifting proudly, 'When I am in Tucson'—she waved her hand towards the dark, menacing desert—'away from all thees, Louis treat me like a princess. And he love me like a whore, and I heem. And when we do eet sends thee blood racing through Catalina, eet ees so good, but then...sometimes...I want to theenk he weel love me when I am old and...but I do not theenk he weel.'

Her voice tapered off, the tone almost whimperingly sad at the end.

Hearing all this tumbling from her lips, Starret felt a pang of sympathy. This, he decided, was a basic, earthy woman crying out against her lot, a woman who wanted a warmth and security she'd probably never known, and thought, at one time, she had found in Bonnard, only to have it brutally shaken by the Frenchman's callous rejection of her yesterday when she was captured by the Lipans—despite having made it clear to her previously that she was on her own if she was captured. She clearly hadn't believed him. And she clearly still wanted to cling to him, despite it—perhaps in the hope she might change him.

'You can't have both, Catalina,' he said heavily. 'One day you'll have to decide on the life and love you really want.'

She gave vent to that natural, throaty

laugh she had. The chat seemed to have relaxed her a little and in an odd way, Starret was glad he had been the instigator of it.

'You theenk so, my brave bull?' she said. 'Cannot I have you just to be a brother who weel protect me, love me—be there for me when I am frightened and lonely and sick, just be there when I am wanting to talk and have your strength to make me feel secure?'

Starret stared into the night moodily. So that was how she viewed him? Her damned brother for God's sake. But in an odd way, he felt flattered. But it didn't help his own edginess, or the reason why he was here.

'Will you get back to camp, damn it?' he snorted. 'I got enough self-pity of my own right now.'

She laughed again, this time mischievously. 'Some day we find out whether you weel by my brother or something else, my beeg bull, *si?*'

Starret glared at her. Catalina was a complex temptress and at the moment bad for him, but he was drawn to her in a way he couldn't quite understand. Like a damned moth to a flame. Oh, sure, there was the sensuality of her, the promise of her body, yet there was something else. And he knew in some strange way, in the end, with all the other problems he had, this one with her would end in terrible heartache. It was the damnedest feeling.

'Catalina, get back to the safety of the camp,' he ordered. 'And leave me to my work.'

She smiled, coyly this time. 'As you weesh, Morgan Starret,' she said.

She went back to the wagons and the fires a hundred yards behind him, inside the perimeter.

Half an hour later a faint rustle to Starret's far left had him tightening up, his senses honing to razor-sharpness.

It could be some critter foraging about, but he instinctively knew he was fooling himself.

He shallowed his breathing as much as he could and lay, hand clasped firmly around the stock of Soam's Winchester.

The cry of agony behind him at the other end of the camp, should have distracted him, set him up, but he did not let it. There was something out there that would take advantage of that. He felt it in his bones. He knew he had to stay still, ignore whatever was going on behind him.

Then rifle fire set up across the perimeter, and sure enough, the Apache he suspected to be in his neck of the woods came out of the night fast, using the racket to cover his move. A silent killer; white war streaks across his cruel visage showing in the faint campfire light, knife held ready for use and bearing down on him not a dozen yards away.

Starret fired the rifle he had in his grip from the hip. The stab of flame lit up the brave's pain-twisted face even more as the lead thumped into him, stopping him momentarily.

But the Lipan, though hurt bad, let out a grunt and came on. And Starret found he hadn't the time to jack in another load so he dropped the rifle and took the striking knife-arm of the brave mid-arc as it came down at him.

Immediately he found himself being forced back to the ground by the impetus of the Apache's charge. But as he went down he managed to get his other big hand around the windpipe of the Lipan and grasped it with steel-trap power. It was then he thought of his Colt, but he didn't alter his grip. The pattern was set.

His hands were used up and he was fighting for his life.

It became a silent death struggle between two men, breath rasping from them in the deep, dark Arizona night, each bent on the other's swift demise.

Starret, grim anxiety gripping him, squeezed with all the force he could muster. The Apache was trying to suck in breath with a weird rasping noise while fighting with desperate strength against the iron grip of Starret's right hand around his throat. And Starret could see the blade of the Lipan's knife was creeping ever nearer to his neck as the brave, with surprising strength, forced down his weaker left arm.

Sweat started to prickle Starret's brow. The damned heathen had the power of the Devil in him, small as he was and hurt like he was. Starret began to fear he would not be able to hold him off much longer.

So he struggled to bring up his right boot, up between the Apache's open legs. Then he punched a vicious kick at the Lipan's genitals, but still holding with grim determination to the Apache's throat. And his kick brought a hissing gasp from the brave. Encouraged by it, Starret punched again, using every ounce of strength he had.

Now the Apache was moaning, writhing —trying to break away. And it was then Starret realized that blood was dripping on to him from the Indian fighting desperately for life above him. The crimson fluid was dropping wetly on to his shirt in a steady patter from the brave's chest wound. Starret could even hear air escaping through it as the Lipan breathed.

He now appreciated that the Indian's strength was starting to flag because of it; became aware that the brave's knife-arm was beginning to tremble under the pressure Starret was imposing on it. And Starret realized the Apache was losing the battle to draw breath through his crumpling windpipe, too. But even though he was hampered by the strength-draining effect of his wound, the Apache still fought mightily to avoid his approaching death, and because of it, Starret strived with greater effort to hasten him towards that end.

In this near-silent battle he watched sweat form on the man's brow, saw desperation and despair come to his black, fierce eyes. Then the Lipan faded suddenly, collapsing to one side. And Starret rolled with him, fighting to gain the dominant position above him, still grasping his throat.

Then the brave quivered and began losing consciousness. Finally the Apache relaxed completely, a choked sigh hissing from him. But Starret held on; crouched over him, his hulking shoulders hunched forward. He'd never strangled a man before. There was no way for him to tell the man was dead. So Starret hung on, staring through the darkness at the man's bulging eyes and out-thrusting tongue.

TEN

Through glaring eyes Starret saw the half-naked Apache on a painted piebald come out of the night. He came galloping past Starret as though he wasn't there. The pony he was on was pounding up choking dust from its unshod hooves.

Almost hidden amongst the cluster of rocks he was in and probably not seen, it brought Starret out of the mad trance

143

he was in—still gripping the strangled Lipan under him like he was. He stared blazing-eyed after the Apache as the brave guided his horse expertly—around the low boulders scattered throughout the inner camp.

Then he saw the brave lash down with his tomahawk at one of the owlhoots who was rising from his blanket, staring bug-eyed and confused into the sudden violence erupting around him in the night. Starret clenched strong teeth as he watched blood and brains splash out of the hole the war axe made before the stricken man dropped lifeless to the ground.

Starret came to his feet, forgetting the brave under him and picked up his rifle. He drew his Colt and lined it up, straight armed. His first shot smacked the rampaging brave off his horse. It was a good shot. Maybe thirty-five yards and it pleased him.

Then he began to realize—while he had fought for his life moments ago—a full-blown ruckus had now developed throughout the camp. Gunfire was stuttering up to a full barrage of staccato shooting from all around the camp perimeter.

As he ran forward Starret could see that

Catalina was crouching under the wagon loaded with the guns, her white face made stare-eyed by the violence and framed in the yellow firelight.

He could see Bonnard was standing near her, firing calmly with his long-barrelled Smith & Wesson at the warpainted Lipans now vomiting with wild shrieks out of the darkness.

And the brief, bitter thought came to Starret: this wasn't like the Apache at all, from what he had heard. He had heard they did not like attacking in the dark night, and he experienced their reluctance years ago during an encounter in the Galiuro Mountains. They usually liked a big moon to light their path. They must have a desperate need for rifles...

The rasping snorting, made by a horse through glared nostrils at full run, had him turning to face the brave bearing down on him, Springfield single-shot trapdoor carbine pointing straight at him. It boomed red-yellow fire and Starret heard the hiss of lead pass his face, so close it burned him. Startled and amazed that the Apache had missed, Starret brought his Colt into play again as the brave turned his mount in its own space to come back, swinging up his war axe.

Though side-stepping, Starret had the satisfaction of seeing his shot knock the Apache out of his blanket saddle. While thumbing back the hammer of his pistol again he watched the brave struggling to his feet. Crouched against the pain of his wound the Lipan began to stagger away. Through his fight fever, energized by the adrenalin pumping through him, Starret could see blood was running redly from a wound in the Apache's groin. He glowered after him, resentment flushing through him. By God, no damned Indian was going to run from him!

For some strange reason Starret hadn't time to discern, he felt cheated by that. Made deadly accurate by the battle-fury in him, his third shot killed the brave—stamping a red hole into his sweat-shiny back, glistening in the light of the campfire he was running past.

Turning away Starret now saw fierce struggles were going on everywhere. He crouched low in the protection of a boulder and feverishly reloaded his Colt. When the sixgun was fully armed again he looked up to see a brave had Bonnard pinned to the wheel of the wagon. His war axe was raised to deal death. Starret could also see Catalina scrambling out from underneath the wagon. She climbed to her feet and began beating the Lipan with puny fists and screaming in Spanish at him as she did.

Starret swung his Colt around, manoeuvred for a side shot, so as not to shoot straight through the Indian's body and maybe kill Bonnard, and to avoid hitting Catalina, too. He still needed Bonnard, he decided.

He fired and the Apache collapsed, the hole in the side of his head spewing blood. As the brave flopped twitching on the ground, Bonnard turned, relieved and grinned towards him. Then he waved his long, shiny gun in ecstatic salute shouting, 'Now you save my life, *mon ami!* We are equal again!'

That's the way you figure it, huh? thought Starret. Yes, there had been the matter of Bonnard saving him from Pheasy's backshot outstanding. He grinned in return, but without feeling any high emotions on the matter. The Rangers wanted Bonnard—he wanted him, too.

Now he could hear a whole lot of urgent talk was flying to and fro between the Lipans, streaking in and out of the firelight like the fearsome demons of Satan.

It wrenched Starret's stare away from Bonnard to search the night. Then, yipping their defiance, the Apaches disappeared into the darkness as quickly as they had come. And suddenly it was quiet...

Deathly quiet...

Slowly time, in that startled night, began to drag out in suspended silence. For what seemed ages nobody moved. The men were looking around, grim-faced, hard-eyed, staring at each other then at the night beyond the perimeter. It appeared everybody was waiting for something to happen, hardly able to comprehend the sudden calm, hardly able to draw breath in case they missed some vital clue that would bring the Lipans storming in on them again.

After long moments and finding his hands beginning to shake a little Starret stepped forward slowly towards the perimeter, regripping his Colt, glaring suspiciously into the night.

'What the hell's goin' on?' he said to nobody in particular.

He turned and stared at Bonnard. The Frenchman, now beside him, shrugged. 'Who knows?' he said.

Then, from the night, the call came, 'Bonnard!'

Visibly tensing, the Frenchman stared into the darkness, wiped the hand with his gun in it across his mouth. Then he whispered to Starret, 'It's Geronimo's interpreter. I know the voice.'

Starret felt his gut knot. So that was why the Lipans had run?

'Come in!' shouted Bonnard.

There was a pause. Still no movement. More silence fell. Then, from the night, the voice speaking guttural English said, 'Geronimo wait for everybody to calm down. Lower guns, please. No more shooting. When done, he say he come in.'

Bonnard looked around him, at the party of men staring nervously into the night, their firearms at the ready.

'You heard the man,' he said.

Eyes still stared, though guns were lowered reluctantly. Glances began to be exchanged, some apprehensive.

Then Bonnard shouted, 'OK now?'

More silence. More time passed, then about twenty Apaches moved like ghosts out of the night, mounted on their wiry ponies. Starret had no trouble picking out Geronimo. Burly, squat—broad face

149

narrowing to a jaw which was full and strong. Watchful eyes that were dark and ever moving—*menacing* eyes. He looked an Apache warrior from the tip of his head to the end of his toenails. Strong. Fierce. Merciless.

The tall warrior beside him spoke again. Clearly he was the go-between.

'Got guns?' he said to Bonnard.

The Frenchman nodded. 'Soon as I see and assess the Lost Vargos, they are yours,' he said. 'You know the deal.'

The warrior nodded. 'Know deal.' He jabbered to Geronimo who shook his head impatiently, waving his right index finger.

The interpreter said, 'Want to see guns before show mine. Not know whether guns are as agreed.'

Bonnard looked surprised. 'Does Geronimo doubt my word?'

The hint of a cynical smile crossed the interpreter's swarthy face. 'For long time Goyathlay[1] doubt all White Eyes' words.'

---

[1] Geronimo's native name. Geronimo was the Mexican nickname for him, derived from Jerome.

150

Bonnard shrugged. 'As you wish.'

Starret watched the Frenchman as he strode past Catalina, who was standing shivering close against the side of the wagon. Bonnard pulled himself up into its canvas-covered interior. He dragged a box to the edge and motioned to the interpreter to take an end. Soon the box was lifted out and lowered to the ground. Bonnard prised open the top, took out a gun and unwrapped the oilpaper wrapping.

Geronimo dismouned and stepped forward and took it, staring at it and turning it in all directions. Despite the grease smeared on it, he worked the mechanism. Meanwhile, Bonnard was dragging out a box of cartridges. He opened them. Again Geronimo inspected.

Then the Apache clenched his fist and beat air with it, nodding his approval. He grunted more guttural words.

The interpreter said, 'Goyathlay say rifles good. Deal is good.'

With that both Apaches turned and strode to their horses and climbed up with muscular agility. Geronimo grunted more words.

The interpreter said, 'We meet again soon, Bonnard.'

'What about the agreement?' called Bonnard. 'Aren't you going to stay and camp with us?'

Completely ignoring him and with a short, harsh command, Geronimo wheeled his horse and the party melted into the night as swiftly as they had come.

Bonnard turned. Starret met the Frenchman's troubled stare. 'I don't like it,' he said. 'What is he attempting, Starret?'

'He's callin' the shots,' Starret said. 'He sayin' it's all on his terms. You're not dealin' with business men now, Bonnard. I wouldn't trust that redskin as far as I could throw him.'

The Frenchman glowered into the night. 'Damn the man for the scoundrel he is if that is the case,' he said. 'I've played it straight down the line with him.'

Starret shrugged. 'Yeah, well, I guess it's wait-see time,' he said. 'The broncos never play anythin' down the line where white men are concerned. They've been bitten too often.'

Bonnard scowled turned and shouted, 'Double the guard.' Then he took Catalina by her arm, gently. 'Come, *cherie*. I am tired.'

Starret watched them disappear into the

wagon they used for their complete privacy. Before she went in, though, Catalina smiled wanly at him, even a little apologetically.

Damn it, what did that mean? Starret scowled. There was no shame in the woman!

ELEVEN

The following day, riding alongside Joe Bell through the steeple hills that surrounded them—the flat bottomland around them sprinkled with giant saguaro, prickly pear, mesquite and yucca—Starret decided the Arizona sun was equally as hot as the Mexican sun and mopped his wet brow. He stared at the close-riding line of riders ahead of him, the vital arms wagon in the middle of the column.

An uneasiness hung like a pall over the men. And when Starret saw Bonnard detach himself from ahead and ride towards them, he spat. As he came close he could see Bonnard's amber gaze was uneasy—a little angry maybe—then he turned his mount to match their walking gait.

He addressed Bell. 'Where the devil is he?' he said.

Joe squinted. 'Geronimo?'

Bonnard stared. 'Of course.' He cut air with his right arm impatiently. 'This isn't the time for flippancy, Joseph.'

Joe shook his head. 'Hell I ain't bein' whut you say,' he said. 'I'm as gut-twitchy as you.'

Bonnard swung his gaze. 'Starret?'

Starret hitched in the saddle. 'Well, like I explained, I trust the Apache about as much as he trusts me,' he said.

Bonnard continued to stare. He appeared to become more irritated. 'And what does that mean?'

Starret shrugged. 'Exactly what it says. I don't trust them at all. Not the broncos, anyway.'

Bonnard shook his head, as if baffled 'I've honoured my end of the bargain and Geronimo has seen the proof of it,' he said. 'As a chief of his tribe he must have some degree of integrity.'

Starret was mildly surprised by the naivety being displayed by Bonnard. He gazed side-long at him. 'Well, for one thing—Geronimo ain't a chief,' he said. 'Medicine man, maybe.'

Bonnard stared at him disbelievingly. 'Of course he is,' he said. 'If he isn't, where do all his warriors come from?'

Starret spat. 'Renegades, like him,' he said. 'They follow him because he's had some pretty rich pickings out of Mexico in his time—one or two whuppings, too. But the good times outweigh the bad, I guess. That's why they join him. But a chief he ain't. Tom Horn tol' me he never was, and never will be, a chief amongst the Apache.'

Joe nodded. 'That's right, so I've heard,' he said. 'They say Cochise never did like him; Victorio puts up with him when it suits him; Nana—that old cuss—goes his own way. Naiche, well he tags along with Geronimo now and again. But a chief? Sorry, Louis, Starret is right.'

The Frenchman stared at each of them. 'I find this incredible.'

Starret wiped his brow free of moisture again. 'You should've asked around, Bonnard,' he said. 'I told you tradin' guns to Apaches is crazy, especially that old timber wolf.'

Bonnard still stared, his square face tight with resentment. 'It is a legitimate business deal.'

Starret sneered, 'Like hell it is. You can't do nothin' legitimate with Geronimo.'

Bonnard's face suddenly became suspicious. 'Again you attack me, Starret,' he said with surprising petulance. 'I'm beginning to think there is too much of a citizen streak in you to make the badman you claim to be. You have a conscience and express it. I always suspect that.'

Starret raised his brows in mock amazement. 'You said you liked a man to be truthful with you, Bonnard.'

Bonnard nodded abruptly, his stare remaining probing. 'There are several ways to the truth, and several results from it.' The Frenchman continued to stare before he shrugged. 'But, this is getting us nowhere. Geronimo should be showing himself.'

'Did you have a meet place?' Starret said.

'Yes.' Bonnard nodded to emphasize, emphatically, his words. 'But I thought, with his appearance last night, it had become unnecessary.'

'They pick places they can trust,' Starret said. 'Places they know they can escape from if things go wrong.'

Bonnard's gaze came up again, quickly.

156

'Why should they think anything should go wrong?'

'Natural distrust,' said Starret. 'An' bad dealin' with whites and Mexes over long years, I guess.'

Bonnard grunted, continued to stare irritably before he urged his horse back up the column briskly to join Catalina, who was riding her favourite palomino.

Joe spat. 'Louis is worried,' he said. 'An' when Louis is worried, I am.' He stared uneasily around him.

Starret nodded. 'I got a prickle up my back, too, but maybe not for the same reasons.'

Joe turned his gaze on to him. 'You seem all-fired concerned about whut the Apache will do with them guns.'

Starret returned Bell's stare. 'Ain't you?'

'Mebbe,' he said. 'But if thet mine's where Geronimo says it is—why, man, I can stand a little gut-tuggin'. I got things you wouldn't believe lined up when I gits my share o' the gold.'

Starret grinned for effect, but to him the whole thing was too serious for that. Somehow, he had to get out of here. Make his report. Stop this deadly trade in guns to Geronimo.

'That right?' he said.

'That's right,' Joe said, and spat more tobacco juice.

Looking forward, Starret noticed they were in a part of the country where the hills drew in to form a narrow gap in the flat land before spreading out again. Uneasily he probed it with grey, steady eyes but, almost before he knew it, Apaches emerged as if grown from the very desert itself and blocked both ends of the narrows.

Alarmed and stern-faced the men immediately formed up, surrounding the wagon with the Winchesters on board, Bonnard rapping orders.

But they were boxed, Starret knew, and an attack by Geronimo, if that's who it was, would see them in deep trouble.

Sure enough, the red devil revealed himself. Starret watched as Geronimo confidently rode forward with his interpreter, detaching themselves from the braves lined up on the rise of ground ahead. At 150 yards they stopped.

'Bonnard!' the interpreter bawled.

The shouted call ebbed away, echoing into the burning hills around them, which stood like eroding steeples under the brassy glare of the sun.

'What is the meaning of this, Geronimo?' the Frenchman called. His voice was firm and his face revealed no fear.

The interpreter bawled, 'Goyathlay is prepared to let you go unharmed—all of you—if you hand over guns.'

Starret saw dark anger rise in the Frenchman's amber eyes. He demanded, 'Has Geronimo no honour? We had a deal.'

Answering the reply Geronimo talked quickly to his interpreter.

'Goyathlay says he is surprised by your reaction—for is it not the white man's way to break his word?' the go-between said. He made no attempt to hide the hard irony in his voice. 'So what is wrong in copying white man, he asks. Goyathlay says that this is always how White Eyes trade. With no honour. So, to make it right, Goyathlay says he will do that, too.'

Starret could see Bonnard was livid. He stared at him. 'Of all the damned humbug!' the Frenchman burst out.

After moments, as if he was collecting himself, he said, 'Tell Geronimo I have dealt with him absolutely honourably. Now tell him to take us to the Lost Vargos mine and we will forget this happened.

That way there will be no blood spilt. No wise man wants that when what is to be gained is better. And tell him I am not as the American. Tell him I come from another place, across the big water where men are honourable.'

Starret could not help but break in, stung a little by the veiled inference all Americans were untrustworthy. 'He ain't goin' to listen to that crap,' he growled.

Bonnard glared for a moment, then ignored him and stared intently at the two Apaches talking together. The interpreter was clearly explaining what Bonnard had said. Then Starret saw Geronimo cut air with his hand.

Again words came. 'No deal, Bonnard,' called the go-between. 'Leave wagon with guns. Ride away. Goyathlay say you not be harmed. Goyathlay keep word on this.'

Bonnard snorted. 'Does he expect me to believe him now?'

The interpreter explained to Geronimo again, then replied, 'Geronimo say he not lie this time. Tell truth on this. Maybe later, when he get to know you better, Goyathlay trust Bonnard more.'

'It is this damned deal I'm concerned about!' Bonnard snarled. 'Tell him it's the

160

mine or nothing. Tell him Bonnard can make threats, too.'

Bonnard turned. Starret met his gaze. Though he could see anger was blazing in the Frenchman's eyes, there seemed to be an underlying calmness in him, triumph almost—as if he felt he would, in the end, control the situation, outwit this ignorant savage.

While the interpreter was talking to Geronimo, Bonnard said, 'I have noted your warnings about Geronimo's lack of integrity, Starret.' He raised his thick brows. 'That may surprise you. And last night I thought deeply about counteracting any deceit—but not because of any scruples about arming him. And my answer is simple, for I will not have a savage dictating to me. These are my precautions: I took them last night.'

He moved to the wagon and swung back the rear flap. Starret narrowed his eyes when he saw the roll of dynamite resting on the cases in the back, primed by a short-fused detonator. Starret blinked. Now that could be powerfully persuasive to a gun-hungry Apache—if he knew what he was looking at!

'I'll blow the damned rifles to Kingdom

Come,' snorted Bonnard, 'if he so much as tries to take them. If he wants them, he pays for them by revealing the whereabouts of the Lost Vargos Mine.'

With that Bonnard turned. 'Geronimo!' he bawled. 'There is something I want you to see.'

Starret could see the interpreter was still trading the words Bonnard had shouted previously. Geronimo's fierce stare turned to Bonnard. When he saw he had the Apache medicine man's attention Bonnard ordered the wagon turned so the rear was on view to him, then pointed to the roll of dynamite.

'That is dynamite,' Bonnard called. 'If it is detonated it will blow all these guns into twisted steel and matchwood instantly. I say again, no mine, no guns.' He turned to the interpreter. 'Tell Geronimo that.'

Even at the distance they were, after the interpreter had spoken, Starret saw Geronimo's face lengthen. The Apache talked animatedly with his interpreter, then glowered their way.

'Goyathlay say Bonnard bluffs,' the interpreter shouted after moments.

Starret saw a mirthless smile cross the Frenchman's broad features. He turned to his men now gathered near the wagon. 'Get ready to run, boys, and take your chances,' he shouted. '*You* know, I don't bluff.'

Then Bonnard pulled out a box of sulphur matches. The owlhoots began to move restlessly, start edging away. Starret saw Geronimo start forward on his pinto pony, his face severe. It was clear he knew exactly what dynamite could do.

Somebody blurted, 'Now hold on there, Mr Bonnard.'

'You got ten seconds, Geronimo,' Bonnard bawled above him. 'One—'

The interpreter was gesticulating furiously as well as speaking as Bonnard counted off.

On eight the interpreter shouted, 'Goyathlay believe Bonnard. Make good trade. Goyathlay now reckon Bonnard's heart is good. Not liar after all.'

Bonnard nodded, his smile broadening. 'Well, thank the noble chief,' said Bonnard, his voice heavy with sarcasm. 'And tell him we'll follow when he leads. And tell him to take his wolves off our backs.'

Once more the interpreter talked away. After seconds Geronimo gave a curt nod and wheeled his pinto.

The interpreter shouted, 'Geronimo agrees,' and rode to catch up with the medicine man.

Starret said, 'He's lyin'. He'll wait 'til you drop your guard, then—' He drew a finger expressively across his tanned, sinewy throat.

Bonnard nodded sagely. 'After this I'm inclined to agree,' he said. 'But I am a gambler, *mon ami*. By gambling I have achieved what I have—not with cards, mark you, but with money...deals...stocks and shares...mining. I like the sting of the uncertainty—the challenge...the battle of wit and nerve it entails. So we play out the trade. We see what destiny throws up for us.'

With that he walked away and mounted up.

Starret stared after him. Joe grinned across at him. 'That's Louis Bonnard, Starret. I ain't seen a play he hasn't won—right from the early days with Quantrill.'

Starret growled. It could well be. And it could well be there is a Lost Vargos Mine. It could be that Bonnard will win through with this deal with Geronimo. The

Apache will get his guns, and Bonnard his gold.

And somehow, Starret thought bleakly, he had to stop it.

TWELVE

Throughout the day the whole bunch of Apaches rode in front making Bonnard's party eat their dust, which brought disgruntled mutterings from the hot crew.

The Apaches took them into the mountains, winding ever higher up obscure, rocky trails, having to make detours to allow for the passage of the wagons. But, even though they did make these adjustments, in places it had still been touch and go.

Nightfall found the two camps quiet, Bonnard's men tired and dirty from the long, arduous trail they had ridden. The fires were glowing in the night and, after a gritty supper, Starret was sitting, brooding over his personal dilemma. One thing stood out in his mind. He had to hang on here. He had to get rid of the guns. And thinking on it, through a stroke of pure luck for him, Bonnard had provided him with the means, introducing the dynamite into the game. But unfortunately, Bonnard had the wagon guarded at all times because of it.

Almost as soon as he had seen the explosive, Starret had formed a plan of sorts early in the day—and despite tossing it over in his mind, as he was doing now, he decided it was as good as he could get it.

After sitting half an hour he pretended to bed down early. He threw down his roll and within moments made as though he had fallen asleep. But the whole time he watched and waited.

Two hours later the camp was quiet, most men tired from the exertions of the day. Only two guards were left standing, one each end of the wagon loaded with the Winchesters. Four more were bellied down on the camp's perimeter. After the events of the last couple of days Bonnard had made clear his distrust of Geronimo. Starret knew his watch was not due for another two hours.

With the descended quiet he licked dry lips. Eyes narrowed he lay surveying the camp all around him. The tired men were sleeping heavily. It had been a hard slog these past days, since leaving the canyon Bonnard used as the owlhoots' roost, and today had been the worst—getting the wagons up the steep trails pushing at heavy wagon wheels under a burning sun—unloading and reloading.

He looked at his pinto tied to the rope picket line, standing alongside the other horses. The line was Bonnard's idea. A military arrangement by a military man. Starret set his lips together in a grim line. All his plan required him to do was to get to the dynamite and blow up the wagon.

Simple. He allowed himself a wry grin. If only it was...

But God knew what carnage it would cause when he did it and it bothered him slightly. Perhaps, with the men lying on the ground, the debris would fly over the top of them. Perhaps there would not be many casualties because of that. His face froze into severe lines in the faint firelight. Perhaps...? Maybe...? He felt angry with himself. The job had to be done, and he had to get down to doing it. He knew the men he fretted about would have no such scruples.

In his book the whole crew were black guilty. They were all willing to trade guns for gold—and in so doing were trading the lives of innocent settlers to satisfy their own greed.

However, there was Catalina...

He had this compulsion working in him to get her out, one way or the other. She was a compelling, alluring woman, with a quaint hint of innocence about her—as though she viewed all life as a game to be played coquettishly, but without malice. He decided she had been drawn into it solely because of her relationship with Bonnard. He felt sure she didn't love him. He was just a meal ticket. Women like Catalina, maybe like many dirt-poor women the world over, would have jumped at this chance for a better life and would use their sexuality to get it.

He stared into the dark night. But choose what she did, or why she did it, he just couldn't leave her here to die—either by the blast from the dynamite, or Geronimo's revenge when the guns were destroyed.

He stared at the wagon she and Bonnard used. The light had been out for some time. He found excitement and elation

168

start to tingle in him. It could all work out. He would saddle the horses first, then he would get hold of the bundle of dynamite, then get Catalina. He would set off the fuse and lob in the sticks of dynamite, and ride like hell...

Easy.

Once more he licked his lips, allowed himself an ironic smile. Easy? Like hell it was! But that was the way he was going to do it.

He slid out of his blankets, each move considered and caution-filled. He got his and Catalina's saddles, then looked around again. It was quiet on the edge of the perimeter. He had previously noted the positions of the guards. Every few seconds he checked, but they were too busy staring away into the night to notice what was going on within the perimeter.

He felt a hint of satisfaction. So far, so good. Too good, maybe...

He reached the picket line. Thirty-seven horses moved restlessly before accepting his familiar scent. He saddled his own horse, then Catalina's palomino.

Then more breath-bated waiting, more searching glances at the perimeter guards. Reassured, he left Catalina's horse tied to the picket line, led his own away towards the gun wagon. The guard at the rear of the conestoga covered him with his rifle suspiciously as he walked up, but lowered it, as if relieved, when he saw who it was.

'What's with the horse, Starret?' he whispered, for some reason Starret was glad of. He wanted all the quiet he could get.

'Bonnard wants me to go out, do a surveillance of the Apache camp,' he breathed. 'He wants to know all that's goin' on up there. You know he likes nothin' left to chance.'

'Hell,' growled the guard quietly, 'you kin have thet chaw.'

Starret managed a thin smile. 'I'm beginnin' to figure it that way, too,' he said.

But with the deceit and speed of a striking diamond-back he brought his Colt off leather, travelled it up swiftly and brought it down with heavy force on to the guard's head. The man was hardly able to react, so complete had been Starret's surprise.

The owlhoot crumpled, went down with a low moan and became still.

Almost immediately, from the other end

of the wagon, the second guard said, 'You all right, Slim?'

Starret did the best he could at miming. 'Here a minute,' he called. 'Think I heard somethin'.'

'Hell, it'll on'y be a minute,' came the reply. 'You know how Bonnard feels about guardin' things—desertin' yore post.'

'Damn it, it's on'y a few seconds I'm askin',' Starret grumbled quietly.

Starret heard the other guard's reluctant footfalls. As he appeared around the edge of the wagon he hit him across the temple with the barrel of his Colt. The man's greasy hat flew off his head, springing ochre dust. He, too, collapsed without a murmur.

Crouched over him, staring into the night, Starret licked his lips once more. It got better by the minute.

He worked fast, pushing the bodies under the wagon, grabbing the roll of dynamite from off the gun cases. Then, with even more thoroughness, he searched the night once again with alert eyes. Still no reaction from the blanket-covered, sleeping men.

Now for Catalina.

As he tied his pinto to the tailboard of the wagon he surveyed the guards on the perimeter. Still no reaction as far as he could see. Satisfied, he edged towards Bonnard's wagon, standing twenty yards away from the gun wagon.

At the canvas flap he hesitated. The sounds of people breathing in heavy sleep came to him. He lifted the flap and sure enough both Bonnard and Catalina were fast asleep in each other's arms. It took Starret back a little to see the embrace. But then, Catalina had made no secret of her feelings for Bonnard, even though he had abandoned her to her fate when the Lipans had captured her. But as he suspected, it could all be a charade on her part.

He hopped up nimbly and went through the flap fast, but already Bonnard was rearing up alertly, reaching for his Smith & Wesson on the pillow beside him, clearly disturbed by the slight sway of the wagon.

'Sta—' he started.

Teeth bared, Starret cut down with his Colt, felt the butt jar on Bonnard's skull. With a sharp cry, the Frenchman fell back across Catalina. Starret hit him again. As he did, Catalina moaned and stirred, snapped open her wonderful green eyes.

'Morgan Starret!' she said. 'What ees—'

He 'shushed' her to silence.

'Follow me,' he hissed. 'Quiet. No time to explain.'

Round-eyed she looked at Bonnard. She struggled from underneath him. As she became erect she became agitated.

'No, no,' she said. 'What have you done to my poor Louis! Have you gone mad?'

'I'm taking you out of this, Catalina,' he hissed.

She stared at him incredulously. 'I do not want to be taken out—as you say, Morgan Starret.'

To Starret's amazement she bent over Bonnard and gathered him in her arms.

Starret stared at her for moments, dumbfounded. What the hell...? He felt anxiety bite at his gut. Damn it, it wasn't supposed to be like this. But he hadn't known how it would be. All he had done was guess, surmise how it was with Bonnard and Catalina. But at base, he just wanted to get Catalina to safety; save her from herself.

So there was no time for argument. He hit her sharply on the chin with his fist. She went limp and he lifted her easily on to his shoulder.

After a moment's hesitation at the canvas flap he slipped out into the sleeping camp.

Within moments he was with his horse.

Working fast now and with less care he undid his horse and leading it ran for Catalina's palomino. At the picket line he untied it and threw the unconscious Catalina over his horse's withers and climbed into the saddle and tugged at the reins on Catalina's palomino. Then he drew his belt knife and slashed the picket line apart and urged the horses into running life.

Knife back in its sheath he tugged at the palomino again. Despite its pulling reaction he managed to reach out the dynamite he had slipped into his saddle-bag. He lit the fuse, kicked flanks and tossed it into the back of the wagon as he rode past. Then, with a wild shout urged the pinto out into the night.

THIRTEEN

Towing Catalina's palomino behind him Starret was well into the draw he had earmarked for his getaway earlier. Its shallow mouth ran almost to the edge of the camp perimeter. Lead from the guard posted there chased him until the roar of exploding dynamite thundered into the night. The flash of the detonation filled the sky with lurid light, illuminating the eroding walls of the draw he rode up. Almost immediately he could hear the shouts and screams of injured men, the shrill neighing of horses still not clear of the area.

His face set in determined lines, climbing ever upwards, he didn't offer to falter, or look back. He ran the horse on, up the draw. After a mile he found its narrow gash opened into level meadowland. He burst out into it, pounding across the 200 yards of dark space and into the pines sprawling up the hill on the other side.

Ten minutes later he came out of the sweet-smelling pines on to a craggy ridge, but with no view because of the darkness—only of what was in the close distance before him. As he picked his way along the rocky razorback he could hear the gunfire behind him was growing from a stuttering to a crescendo of steady fire. Geronimo, he guessed, must have realized what had happened and was moving in...

Still hanging limp across the withers

of the pinto he rode he heard Catalina moan. She started to move. Seeing it he brought the horse to a halt, climbed down, ground-hitched her palomino, and lifted her down. It thrilled him to feel her narrow, unsupported waist beneath his big, strong fingers.

'Do you think you can ride, Catalina?' he said.

She staggered, holding her jaw when he let go of her. Though she was clearly still bemused she said, 'Where ees Louis? What have you done?' Her big eyes came up to gaze at him. They looked sad and hurt. 'You heet me, Morgan Starret,' she said, her voice rising as she became more conscious. 'Why eees that? What ees happening to us? Why are you doing thees? Tell me.'

Starret knew he couldn't waste time talking here. He had to get on to Tucson, see Catalina safe, make his report, get men out to clear up what he had started back there. Though the Ranger force only amounted to maybe fifteen men under the leadership of Captain Burton C. Mossman, willing posses could usually be enlisted and sworn in quickly.

Ignoring her demands he said, 'Get

on your horse, Catalina. We're ridin' to Tucson.'

The Mexican beauty stared at him defiantly, resentfully. 'I go nowhere weethout Louis,' she said hotly. 'Where ees he?'

Starret stared at the now quickly recovering fireball before him. It was becoming apparent, as her head cleared, she was becoming more agitated by the second because of the predicament she found herself in. And her attitude puzzled him. Sure, she had a right to be angry about him hitting her. But somewhere along the line—regarding her relationship with Bonnard—he must have read it wrong. Or maybe he just didn't know women well enough to judge their actions, moods, or fealties. He had been told by his father they could be mighty different from a man's when it came right down to it.

'Understand this, Catalina,' he snorted, 'Bonnard doesn't give a damn for you. You know that. And I've just blown up his gun wagon. When the Apaches get to know—which I already think they have—they will be hopping mad.' He grabbed her roughly, for there was no time for niceties. 'You're comin' with me

177

and there's an end to it.'

As he spoke, far below, Starret could hear the sound of gunfire was hotting up. A regular battle was being established, it seemed. It was maybe as he had anticipated—that most of the debris from the explosion must have gone over the heads of the owlhoots still prone. They may have been concussed a little, but with Geronimo howling down upon them, hell-bent on vengeance, the shock of that concussion would be forgotten in the need to preserve their lives.

He felt Catalina twist out of his grasp with a cat-like snarl. She began running towards her palomino standing patiently nearby, the reins trailing on the ground. It was cropping the short grass between the rocks.

'I go to be weeth Louis,' she shrilled. 'I die weeth heem. You weel not stop me Morgan Starret.'

Starret bounded across the space to her and dragged her off the palomino. 'Damn it,' he raged, 'you're stayin' with me. You'll get killed down there.'

She began to beat at his chest and scream. 'You are not my lover,' she bawled. 'You are not my man! You are not even my brother any more. You are a traitor!'

Stung by her words and realizing again he had no choice, he hit her once more. She sagged, dazed, against him giving vent to a sighing cry. He felt angered by the need to. It went against every grain of decency in him. But, damn it, a sore jaw was a better bet than lead poisoning. She was crazy now, he tried to assure himself, but she would thank him later—when she was more rational. Her feelings for Bonnard could, for sure, only be infatuation.

Startling him came another staccato of shuddering explosions from below. More dynamite...? It instantly startled Catalina's palomino causing it to run, neighing shrilly, into the night.

Cursing, Starret gave chase for several yards before stopping and fuming at the night as it closed in on the pale-yellow, running horse. He heard it crashing through the brush, pounding into the distance. Well, thank God his own pinto was of sterner stuff. When he returned, it was standing patiently in the trees awaiting him.

Without ceremony he hoisted Catalina

across the withers once more and climbed up. Hard determination filled him. She was going to Tucson whether she liked it or not!

He looked about him, shutting out the noise of the renewed gunfire below him. In the light of the pale half-moon edging over the skyline east he could see the ridge fell away. More warmer, level ground must be down there somewhere.

He put the buckskin down into the pines, again their pungent smell pleasing to his nostrils. And oddly, on the whole, he felt good. He had stopped the gun shipment going to Geronimo; had stopped Bonnard and his men—what remained of them—and left them fighting for their lives. From the sound of it, though, they were maybe even giving Geronimo a lesson for they were all hardcases.

However, not a bad night's work for one man in borrowed clothes and riding a hard-won, fighting pinto.

As he rode down the hillside it became more rugged and under the canopy of the pines it was dark—dark enough to make progress on this rough ground hazardous. Annoyed at having to rein down on the pinto and pick his way gingerly down the steep incline, Catalina did not help matters by waking up again. She recovered quickly, though she still hung over the withers.

She moaned accusingly, 'My jaw...eet hurts.' Then she glared fiercely up at him. She said venomously, 'You are thee man weeth two faces. You are *not* my brother—nor my brave bull any more! You are like most *gringos* I know—hard and brutal. Louis would not treat me like thees. Louis ees gentleman, a *patrón.*'

Starret became disgruntled by her childish behaviour. He growled, 'He is, huh? Well, understand this, Catalina, you leave me no choices.' He glowered down at her. 'Now shut up bitching, will you? Can't you see I'm saving you from yourself, damn it!'

From her clearly uncomfortable position he assisted her, as she struggled to do so herself, to sit astride in front of him. Then, turning, she gave him that haughty look. 'I do not need you to save me, Morgan Starret. I am thee woman of Louis Bonnard.'

Then, taking him totally by surprise, her eyes staring and vicious, she reached and clawed her fingers down his gaunt, dust-streaked cheeks.

Galvanized by the pain Starret swayed

to avoid her, tugging involuntarily at the reins. The pinto fought the sudden wrench of the bit and whistled and sidestepped nervously on the precarious slope. Then, with a shrill neigh, lost its footing.

It toppled, fighting to stay upright on the unreliable surface of the incline. And Starret found himself—no matter how he fought to hold on—being catapulted off the saddle and into dark space, Catalina a flurry of skirt and slim agility in the corner of his eye, going the other way. She was striving to hang on to the horse's neck.

Now Starret found himself rolling and bouncing down the steep hillside jarring through brush and against rock, then he smacked into a rearing boulder that appeared from nowhere in the night. Stars flew across his vision before he plunged into deep blackness.

When he came round he found it was his turn to be across the withers. Hanging down and bumping against the horse, his head was throbbing fit to burst. He could feel the dry cake of blood in his hair and down the side of his face. And his arms were pinioned to his sides by Harlon Pheasy's lariat.

From above him, Catalina said, 'Do not try to do anytheeng, Morgan Starret. Eef you do, Catalina weel keel you.'

As the haze cleared, Starret turned his head up as best he could to see the muzzle of his own Colt pointing at his head. Despite his situation he found an ironic humour bubbling up in him. Fine chance of trying a damned thing with this hemp around his arms.

'Where are you taking me, Catalina?' he demanded.

'To thee hideout een thee canyon,' she said calmly. 'There I wait for Louis. He weel know what to do.'

The streak of black humour in Starret died as swiftly as it had arisen when the consequences of being at Bonnard's mercy grew large in his mind. 'Think about it, Catalina,' he said harshly. 'Ride with me into Tucson. I will speak for you. In any case, Bonnard is probably dead. Give yourself the chance of a decent life.'

Catalina laughed throatily. 'Weeth Morgan Starret?'

Starret found himself resenting the half-mocking tone in her voice. 'Damn it, why not?'

Catalina made a disparaging noise before

183

saying, 'The Apache weel not keel Louis. Louis weel leeve and he weel keel you, Morgan Starret, for what you do to Catalina.'

Desperate anger began to fill Starret. He urged, 'Damn it, woman, even if he is alive, Bonnard is finished in Arizona. And he'll take you down with him.'

'I take my chances weeth Louis,' snapped Catalina. 'Now, eef you do not stop talking Catalina weel heet you weeth thee gun, *si?*'

Starret lapsed into silence because he believed Catalina would do just as she said she would. In this situation he had to stay alert; look for the one chance to get in control again. The last thing he wanted to be was unconscious.

As they rode uncomfortably on, the night faded and a cool dawn came in, mist rising out of the deep hollows below the ridge they were now on. By now the jolt of the horse under Starret had set up a nagging ache in his ribs and his head still throbbed from the blow it had received from the rock he had collided with.

A quick, straining glance up told him they were coming into familiar ground. They weren't far from the canyon hideout.

There were landmarks he had earmarked on the first ride there. It was clear, too, Catalina was at home here in these surroundings. She picked her way surely through the maze of hills.

At a stream she stopped and eased her body off the pinto. Then he felt her grasp the bonds binding his chest and arms. Without ceremony she pulled him off the horse. He crashed to the ground and lay on his back, pinioned and looking up at her. He could now see the green-blue discoloration on her jaw where he had hit her. And it was then he wondered just how she had got him on to the horse. Catalina was proving to be a tough cookie. Even so...

'Forget this, Catalina,' he said to her. 'While you have the chance.'

Her ripe, full lips curled up into a sneering grimace. 'You forget eet, *gringo*,' she said. 'Soon we weel be at the canyon.'

'Bonnard won't be there,' he said.

While she spoke Catalina was searching in the saddle-bags. 'He weel be there and he weel keel you.'

He appreciated what she was looking for when she brought out the jerky he had kept in his bags since leaving the canyon, just in case things developed like they had done. She cut a piece and stuck it in his mouth. He chewed, wishing for water to soften it. It was as if she had read his thoughts. She got out his enamel cup, filled it at the stream, satisfied her own thirst and returned with a drink for him.

As he chewed, staring up at her, he said, 'Bonnard doesn't give a damn for you, Catalina. He was prepared to sacrifice you to Geronimo back there. What kind of a man does that?'

She looked at him, her eyes flashing, but clearly she was stung afresh by the reminder.

'He make no secret of eet,' she said then, defensively. 'He warned Catalina that was maybe how eet might be. But he would have saved me, I know.' She pressed her ample bosom and nodded solemnly. 'Een here I know. Een my heart.'

Starret said quietly, 'It was me that pulled you out of that one, Catalina, not Bonnard. Don't you think I don't feel anythin' for you, too?'

Her green gaze was quickly on to him, as if searching his beard-stubbled, dust-stained face for insincerity.

Then she said softly, '*Si*, I theenk you do. And once my brave bull was een Catalina's heart, too—as my brother, until you dishonoured us. Louis in particular. To heem honour ees everything. He gave you hees trust. You have thrown eet back een hees face.' Her Latin temperament flared up. 'And for that I spit on you!'

And she did and it angered Starret to feel the spittle running down his face.

She flounced away from him, her Titian hair, though tousled and unkempt, glistening brilliantly in the sun. Her clothes were dirty too, from the rough night they had spent together, but her figure still moved provocatively under them. Nothing would hide that.

Though angered, Starret ate in silence, lying there in extreme discomfort. After a short time Catalina came back to him.

'We go, Morgan Starret,' she said.

Starret eyed her from his prone position. 'I have to get on my feet,' he said.

She moved behind him. He felt her hands in the grooves where his arms were clamped against his chest by the rope. She grabbed the tight hemp there. She heaved. And he was surprised by her strength. With the help of his legs and pushing against her while she hoisted he came erect.

'So far, so good, I guess,' he said. He grinned wolfishly at her, though why he couldn't figure. He was in no position to merit it and he was scheming madly on how to get out of the situation.

But seeing the grin and as if on impulse, she stepped forward, took a small handkerchief from her skirt pocket and wiped his face free of her spittle. A moment of tenderness came to her eyes.

'I am sorry, Morgan Starret,' she said. 'Eet ees not like Catalina to do that.'

'Sure,' he said. 'I guess you want me on the horse now, huh?'

He felt a tinge of hope stir in him. He might be able to swing something while they struggled between them to get him on the horse. What, he didn't know. There just might have been something he could use...

But he watched her face alter, take on a hardness he hadn't seen before. 'You theenk I am crazy?' she said. 'You walk, Morgan Starret. Eet ees not far to the canyon from here.'

Stung by the fact that he was being pushed around by a woman he glowered at her while she prepared to climb on to the pinto. It was as she got astride, it happened; the one thing he hadn't figured on. Pheasy's pinto kicked up wildly and started to sunfish around madly and prance off stiff legs. And clearly Catalina was not ready for it.

With a squeal, she toppled off, backwards. She fell heavily and lay, clearly dazed and winded by the impact. Elated by the turn of events Starret looked around him anxiously. This was his one chance. But he had only his legs; his arms were pinioned.

And as he floundered in his mind it dawned on him why the pinto had baulked at her. As had been proved before, the horse had a one-man temperament. But why hadn't it rebelled before? The answer came equally as quickly. He had been on its back then.

He plunged at a fast run into the trees all around the clearing they were in. If the pinto remained fractious, Catalina was afoot, too, unless she tamed the animal.

But there was more desperate need for him: he had to find something sharp, something to free him of his bonds.

FOURTEEN

He ran for the densest part of the trees, ignoring the whip of the branches against his face. He had to get to a rock, something with enough sharpness to sever the bonds holding him. Then, at least, he would be free of their crippling restraint.

It wasn't long before he saw a soaring pillar with a rough, knife-like edge.

His chest heaving painfully against the tight bonds he backed up to it and began to rub, flexing his knees up and down as he pressed against the rock. There was one part of his bonds that was loose, near his left hand, loose enough to get the edge in and working on the hemp.

Under the sun that was moving higher into the sky, sweat began to roll off his brow and into his eyes, stinging them. But he worked relentlessly. He didn't know what time he had. He didn't know whether Bonnard had survived back in the hills, or where the Frenchman was now. And Catalina had his gun and horse.

He felt one of the bond strands part, then another until the tightness went from the rope and it dropped, snake-like around his ankles.

His feelings of helplessness dropping off him like a cloak he rubbed life into his arms and body, all the time listening to the forest noises. Then there was a crashing in the trees nearby. Unbelievably, Catalina came out through them running.

By the time she saw him she was almost upon him. Without ceremony he took her down under him in a football tackle. The jolt as she hit the ground caused the gun in her hand to go off. The noise racketed through the steeple hills, sending up the birds in an alarmed chorus.

Then he wrenched it out of her grasp, holstered it and hauled her up before shoving her forward unceremoniously.

'Back to the horse, Catalina,' he rasped harshly. 'And no tricks. I'm not in the mood for them any more.'

She pouted at him, her green eyes ablaze, before she walked back up the hillside—erect, proud, provocative.

As he followed her Starret ejected the empty shells in the Colt and introduced fresh loads. But there had been one shot.

It could have alerted Bonnard—if he was still alive—or Geronimo, maybe on his way to the canyon to pillage what he could and ravage the women left there.

Starret grinned to himself but with little mirth. He was letting his mind run off again. It was just too much speculation. What he had to do was to get to headquarters and as quickly as he could while things were hot. Simple. No if, buts, or maybes.

He found when he reached the place where he had ran from Catalina, the pinto hadn't strayed far and it nickered when it recognized him. On the way up there Catalina hadn't spoken at all and he was glad of that. He coaxed the pinto to him and thankfully he climbed on to the back of the horse and waved an impatient arm. 'Up here, Catalina,' he ordered. 'Any more tricks and I'll really lay you out.'

He was angry with her—had every reason to be, damn it. She still did not speak, just pouted and looked at him sulkily.

He urged the pinto down the hillside, heading east towards Tucson. His mind was a jumble of thoughts. What had happened with the Rangers and the county police force since the shootings at the prison van in the pass? They must have a posse out...it might still be out.

And what of Bonnard? Had he survived? There had been the string of explosions after the initial deadly stutter of gunfire last night. Had Bonnard had one more trick up his sleeve—a trick he, Starret, didn't know about? It was possible. He growled. But it was getting nowhere, this speculation. He liked to deal with things as he found them—not chew over how they might be.

He came out into the meadowland below without caution, for he figured there could be nothing to bother him yet, but the crack of the rifle from the trees ahead and the hum of the lead inches over his head had him swinging the pinto back into the trees he had just broken out of.

A raging cacophony of shots followed him. It set Catalina screaming and grasping hold of the pinto's flying mane as Starret put the beast into a flat run.

But emerging from the trees they were running for there were a line of riders. And Starret immediately realized he had been steered towards them. He recognized some of them. Bonnard's men.

He stared at them for moments before he swung the pinto round, only to find Bonnard emerging from the other side with another line of owlhoots. Starret brought the pinto to a halt. Seeing it the Frenchman spurred forward until he was only twenty yards from him.

But it was Catalina who spoke. Starret felt her body stiffen against him. 'Oh, Louis,' she sighed. 'You have come. I knew you would.'

Bonnard smiled at her, then held up a hand. 'A moment, *cherie.*' He turned to Starret. 'Well, you have nowhere to go, *mon ami,*' he said. 'Please, throw down your gun.'

Starret remained seated, holding Catalina to him, his Colt held in his right hand.

'How did you do it, Bonnard?' he demanded.

Bonnard smiled again. 'Yes,' he said. 'I thought you would ask for I did not tell you the rest of my plans, did I? Sticks of dynamite, *mon ami,* thrown in amongst semi-wild ponies with savages on their backs can have a devastating effect. And it was remarkable how many of my men survived your fireworks disply.' He swept

194

an expressive arm around the meadowland. 'As you can see.'

Starret had already counted over fifteen men.

'Geronimo?' he said.

Bonnard smiled. 'I have a feeling he will be back,' he said. 'But I will be ready for him.'

Starret glowered. 'I guess a coyote has less tricks than you, Bonnard,' he said.

'Skill, *mon ami*,' corrected Bonnard. 'I like to think it is skill. Now, let Catalina go.'

'If I don't?'

Bonnard smiled, creasing his plump cheeks. 'You cannot hold her forever,' he said. 'And I have plenty of time. But there is one thing I must ask you: why did you do it? You could have been a rich man, along with all of us.'

Starret brought himself erect. 'I am an Arizona Ranger, Bonnard, and you are under arrest for murder and the attempted illegal selling of arms to the Apache,' he said.

With that out Starret lifted his head proudly. There seemed little point in hiding the fact any more. But he felt a little ludicrous making such a statement with fifteen or more hostile guns trained on him.

Bonnard leaned back, stylish in his frock coat and cravat and handsome Smith & Wesson in his hand. He laughed softly. After moments he said, 'Well, I must admit, you have nerve enough for ten men, Starret. Pity. I think you and I could have made quite a team. You would have needed a little training, of course. However, you will have the pleasure of knowing I will give it to you clean. No Soam stuff, though you deserve it.'

Bonnard raised his gun and Starret blinked, tightened his grip around the walnut handle of his own Colt. His brain raced for answers. Then it came.

'Sort of a Mexican standoff, ain't it, Bonnard?' he rasped. 'What about Catalina?'

Bonnard's amber eyes became round, curious. 'What about her?'

'Ain't it occurred to you that you'll have to go through her to get to me?' Starret said.

'Oh, yes,' the Frenchman said. 'It had occurred to me.'

He raised the Smith & Wesson. There was a hint of regret in his amber gaze.

'Sorry, *cherie*,' he said. 'But as I have always tried to explain to you—if needs be....'

Catalina's gasp was stark on the bright morning. 'You would keel me, Louis? After we have loved each other so much?'

But Starret had erupted into frantic motion. His desperate bluff had been called. No way could he have sacrificed Catalina. He threw her from the horse and kicked the pinto forward, sent it cannoning into Bonnard's midnight black.

Startled by the abrupt move Bonnard fired wildly. Starret felt hot lead fan his cheek. He grasped Bonnard's gun and wrenched it out of his hand before yanking on the Frenchman's coat and swinging himself on to the back of Bonnard's big stallion. Now holding his left arm in an iron grasp across Bonnard's neck, Starret pressed the Colt to the Frenchman's temple.

'Right, *mon ami*,' he hissed with vicious venom, 'tell your men to back off, or, swear to God, I'll blow your brains out.'

To Starret's surprise a laugh broke from Bonnard. 'You are truly a man of action, Starret,' he said. 'What a pity you took to the law.'

With that the crazy fool attempted to swing round, but already Starret's gun was firing. Blood flew, spattering into Starret's face and he felt Bonnard go limp against him.

He threw Bonnard from him, a lifeless figure. Bonnard had once told him that he never bluffed. Maybe he should have told Bonnard that, on some occasions—neither did he.

He became aware of lead humming around him. Frantically, he dropped off the big stallion and pulled it down. He hunkered behind it staring madly at the owlhoots surrounding him.

But there were other guns firing, he realized, distracting the owlhoots from gunning him down. Then he could see other riders coming out of the trees...

FIFTEEN

Starret then realized Catalina was whimpering on the ground on all fours nearby, staring at Bonnard lying dead, half his head blown off by Starret's lead.

198

Abandoning the cover of the prone stallion Starret ran to her and pulled her down into the tall grass and went down with her. Peering up he saw two men were riding down on him, ignoring the other riders coming out of the trees, shooting. One was Clute James. Starret couldn't mistake his sandy hair and rough features, the other was Joe Bell.

The boom of Bell's Sharps echoed across the meadowland. Starret heard the hum of its lead hissing past his head and instinctively he almost tried to burrow his body into the ground beneath him to avoid it. He had seen the effect of Bell's firing before, and the deadliness of it. Perhaps excitement, something, had caused Bell to miss this time—maybe the rock of the running horse he was sat upon.

It didn't matter for Starret saw they'd got to within twenty-five yards of him. Clute James had his Colt out and aiming. Starret steadied his arm and fired a split-second before him. James seemed to hang up in the saddle for a moment, then collapsed out of it, rolling over and over before he came to a standstill. There he lay moaning and holding his gut.

Starret could now see Bell was still trying

to reload his Sharps as he went past. Without compunction, Starret followed him, taking steady aim and fired. Bell rocked in the saddle, then bent forward and hung on, raking the sides of his horse with cruel spurs, sending it towards the trees. He almost made it before fire from the men who had appeared from nowhere cut him down.

As quickly as the firing had flared up it began to die, became sporadic. It was then Starret saw Captain Mossman at the head of four men come riding towards him. Meanwhile, members of what had to be a big posse were chasing Bonnard's hardcases into the hills. Mossman rode erect atop his fine horse, black dome-topped hat square on his head, wide-set eyes staring steadily at him out of his long head, his firm, generous mouth smiling slightly.

Starret rose, bringing Catalina up with him. She was still numbly staring at Bonnard's motionless figure.

Mossman said, 'Before you ask, I'll tell you, Starret. When the prison van didn't arrive at Yuma we formed a posse and picked up the trail in the pass. With difficulty we followed it until it brought us to the robbers' lair, the narrow canyon back yonder. With a little persuasion we got the ladies there to tell us when they thought their menfolk would be back, then waited. Well, to cut it short, we'd just about given up when we heard the shots. It was enough for us. Enough to bring this whole posse of thirty sound men to this location to find out what the commotion was about.'

Starret nodded. 'Well, sir, I guess you couldn't have timed it better,' he said. 'I'd figured myself a goner.'

Mossman nodded. 'It'll give me great pleasure to read your report, Morgan,' he said. Then he ran his glance over the clothes Catalina had loaned him—the small black hat, the bolero jacket, conchoed chaparejos, the woollen shirt and trousers. 'Interesting suit,' he added. 'Put that in your report, too.' Then he turned to the men behind him. 'Well, let's go finish them off, boys.' Then he doffed his hat to Catalina. 'And 'day to you, ma'am—whoever you are.'

Now Starret found Catalina slumping against him. 'Oh, my brave bull,' she sighed. 'I am so tired. Was Louis really going to keel me?'

Starret nodded. 'You still ain't figured it out, have you, Catalina? Yes, damn it, he was!' But he could see the tears in her eyes as she looked up at him and something grabbed his heart.

'Why?' she whimpered. 'He said he loved me.'

Starret shook his head. 'Well, I ain't got an answer to that, Catalina,' he said. 'The man was jest too blamed deep for me, I guess.'

He felt her body press on to him. 'Some day,' she said, 'I weel not see you as a brother any more. Can you wait, my *gringo* bull?'

Starret sighed, smiled, felt light as a feather—though God knew why he did for he was taking on a she-cat here and he knew it. He took her chin at its point in his thick fingers. He stroked the bruise there with as much gentleness as he was capable of.

He said, 'Sure I can wait, if I'm forgiven.'

The green eyes came up, alluring, provocative and puzzled. 'The man who has saved my life twice ees asking for forgiveness?'

'I did hit you twice,' Starret pointed out.

202

She stepped away from him, eyes wide. 'Thee *gringo!*' Her laughter tinkled across the meadow, her misery seemingly forgotten. 'Sometimes they are so stupid! Do you not know I deserved eet, and that eet ees up to thee man to do sometheeng about it?' She laughed more before turning away, her hands akimbo.

Feeling his blood surging, Starret took her by the waist and pulled her round and to him. 'No,' he said, 'I didn't know. But I learn fast.'

When he had kissed her and she had melted for a moment in his arms she broke away with a giggle and went towards Bonnard. 'But first,' she said, 'I must kees my Louis goodbye.'

Stunned for a moment by the slightly ghoulish desire, Starret shook his head and allowed a grim smile to form on his lips. Some woman, he thought, before checking and filling the empty chambers in his Colt.

It seemed, for sure, he was destined for an interesting life with Catalina Gomez there to share it...

The publishers hope that this book has given you enjoyable reading. Large Print Books are especially designed to be as easy to see and hold as possible. If you wish a complete list of our books, please ask at your local library or write directly to: Dales Large Print Books, Long Preston, North Yorkshire, BD23 4ND, England.

This Large Print Book for the Partially sighted, who cannot read normal print, is published under the auspices of

THE ULVERSCROFT FOUNDATION